DON'T TELL

A JACK RYDER NOVEL

WILLOW ROSE

BOOKS BY THE AUTHOR

HARRY HUNTER MYSTERY SERIES

- ALL THE GOOD GIRLS
- RUN GIRL RUN
- NO OTHER WAY
- NEVER WALK ALONE

MARY MILLS MYSTERY SERIES

- WHAT HURTS THE MOST
- YOU CAN RUN
- YOU CAN'T HIDE
- CAREFUL LITTLE EYES

EVA RAE THOMAS MYSTERY SERIES

- DON'T LIE TO ME
- WHAT YOU DID
- NEVER EVER
- SAY YOU LOVE ME
- LET ME GO
- IT'S NOT OVER
- NOT DEAD YET

EMMA FROST SERIES

- ITSY BITSY SPIDER
- MISS DOLLY HAD A DOLLY
- RUN, RUN AS FAST AS YOU CAN

- Cross Your Heart and Hope to Die
- Peek-a-Boo I See You
- Tweedledum and Tweedledee
- Easy as One, Two, Three
- There's No Place like Home
- Slenderman
- Where the Wild Roses Grow
- Waltzing Mathilda
- Drip Drop Dead
- Black Frost

JACK RYDER SERIES

- Hit the Road Jack
- Slip out the Back Jack
- The House that Jack Built
- Black Jack
- Girl Next Door
- Her Final Word
- Don't Tell

REBEKKA FRANCK SERIES

- One, Two...He is Coming for You
- Three, Four...Better Lock Your Door
- Five, Six...Grab your Crucifix
- Seven, Eight...Gonna Stay up Late
- Nine, Ten...Never Sleep Again
- Eleven, Twelve...Dig and Delve
- Thirteen, Fourteen...Little Boy Unseen
- Better Not Cry
- Ten Little Girls
- It Ends Here

MYSTERY/THRILLER/HORROR NOVELS

- Sorry Can't Save You
- In One Fell Swoop
- Umbrella Man
- Blackbird Fly
- To Hell in a Handbasket
- Edwina

HORROR SHORT-STORIES

- Mommy Dearest
- The Bird
- Better watch out
- Eenie, Meenie
- Rock-a-Bye Baby
- Nibble, Nibble, Crunch
- Humpty Dumpty
- Chain Letter

PARANORMAL SUSPENSE/ROMANCE NOVELS

- In Cold Blood
- The Surge
- Girl Divided

THE VAMPIRES OF SHADOW HILLS SERIES

- Flesh and Blood
- Blood and Fire
- Fire and Beauty
- Beauty and Beasts
- Beasts and Magic
- Magic and Witchcraft

- Witchcraft and War
- War and Order
- Order and Chaos
- Chaos and Courage

THE AFTERLIFE SERIES

- Beyond
- Serenity
- Endurance
- Courageous

THE WOLFBOY CHRONICLES

- A Gypsy Song
- I am WOLF

DAUGHTERS OF THE JAGUAR

- Savage
- Broken

Not a word was spoken in the cold darkness. They didn't have to say anything. The small group of people rushing across the snow all knew they just had to get the job done. Once it was over, they'd go back to living their lives. Nothing would ever be the same after that night; they all knew it wouldn't, but they were going to try. They were all going to try and pretend like it hadn't happened.

The body they were carrying was heavy, and their boots sank deep into the snow because of the weight. It wasn't heavy just because of the guilt it came with, but also because of the size. As they reached the door, they paused as if they were gathering the strength to embark upon this journey.

Getting inside didn't bring warmth and comfort to any of them, only temporary shelter from the biting wind. Nothing could remove the feeling of ice-cold fear that was sliding down their backs.

As they dumped the body, the sound of it hitting the bottom made them want to throw up. The lid was slammed shut, and finally, someone spoke the only two words that were said between them on that fateful night—two words that would haunt them all for the rest of their lives.

"Don't tell."

PROLOGUE

MAGGIE VALLEY
THE GREAT SMOKY MOUNTAINS
NORTH CAROLINA
JANUARY 26TH, 2019

"**D**ad, have you seen Benjamin?"

Penelope Rutherford stood at the top of the stairs looking down at her father in the hallway. As always on Sunday mornings, he had been out to grab the local paper, *The Mountaineer*, from the driveway and was holding it in his hand as the words fell. He barely looked up from the cover story.

"Did you hear me, Dad?" his daughter said impatiently. "Dad?"

His eyes finally let go of the story of how they were still struggling to raise money to rebuild *Ghost Town in the Sky*, the old amusement park in their town that used to attract tens of thousands of tourists in the summertime, but had been closed down for decades.

"I am sorry. I was somewhere else. What was that about Benjamin?"

"Is Benjamin downstairs? He's not up here. He's not in his bed."

Pastor Charles Rutherford took a deep breath and glared at his daughter in front of him. Looking at her often filled him with such deep worry. She was almost too beautiful for this cruel world.

"He's not down here either. Are you sure he's not still sleeping in his bed? He never usually gets up this early."

Charles threw out his arms. Outside, it was snowing as it had been all night. The roads were packed with cars heading for Cataloochee to ski, even though it was barely dawn yet. Church would be next to empty this morning due to this weather.

"But his bed is empty," she said. "It looks like no one has slept in it at all. I don't think he's been in it all night."

"I don't have time for this; I should be getting ready," the pastor said and shook his head. "Penny, where is your brother if he isn't in his bed?"

"I don't know," Penny replied, whining slightly. "That's why I'm asking you. I haven't seen him since last night."

"What's going on?"

Beatrice Rutherford came out from the kitchen, bringing the smell of pancakes and coffee with her. "Charles? Penny? Why aren't you dressed yet?"

"Your son isn't in his bed," Charles snapped. "Apparently, he's been out all night."

The Rutherfords had two sons, but Charles didn't have to say which one he was talking about; his wife knew right away that it had to be Benjamin, the youngest of the two.

Beatrice went pale, then lowered her eyes like she was the one who had been disobedient. Her husband pointed the paper at her.

"If that boy of yours isn't in church today, I'll have my way with him."

"Please don't, Dad; I'm sure he's just...sleeping at a friend's house," Penny said and came down the stairs. Charles spotted deep fear in her young eyes as she was probably regretting having told him anything. Being only a year and a half apart, the two siblings usually stuck together and kept each other's secrets.

Her father turned to face her, a small snort leaving him. "He's with her again, isn't he? Isn't he?"

Penelope didn't answer. Charles felt the unmistakable wave of rage rush through him when thinking about the two of them together.

"I'm serious, Beatrice," he said addressed to his wife. "This has to have consequences. I am sick of that boy doing whatever he wants. As long as he lives under my roof, I want him to follow my rules. He knows how important Sunday mornings are to me and having my family there. I am the pastor of this church. How will it look if one of my family members isn't there? It will look like I can't even control my own son. That's what they'll say; you know that."

"I do," she said and locked eyes with her daughter for a brief moment. Penelope came closer and clung to her mother.

Charles looked out the dark window, then thought to himself that maybe the kid had just gotten himself stuck at her place and was unable to come back due to the weather. He'd have to give him a lesson on how to use the expensive cell phone that Charles had bought him for his seventeenth birthday.

"I'll go look for him," Charles said. "I'll just have to skip the pancakes this morning. That boy of yours better have a darn good excuse for me to have to go fetch him in this weather and miss my Sunday pancakes and coffee before church. It better be good; I tell ya."

Charles grabbed his thick winter coat by the door, then put on his boots. Outside the door, he could hear the wind howling as the snowstorm raged. He braced himself for the cold shock when he grabbed the doorknob and realized the door wasn't closed properly and the screen door was unlatched and wavering in the wind. Snow had blown in between the screen and the door, and some of it had even made it into the front hallway, where it had melted and left a small puddle.

Charles pushed the door open and went out on the wooden porch. The sun hadn't risen yet, and he could barely see anything. Snowflakes danced in the porch light, and he could hear the crackling creek that ran through their property.

"Benjamin?" he called out, thinking he should at least search the property before he went to her house. "Are you out here, Benjamin?"

His words never returned to him. They seemed to be swallowed by the quiet that came with the snow.

"Benjamin? Benjamin Rutherford!"

In the dim light from the approaching dawn, he spotted his oldest son, Charles Junior's truck parked in the driveway. Benjamin often used his brother's truck when going somewhere, but apparently not today. There were no footprints in the driveway after the heavy snowfall the night before. No fresh tracks were leading to or from the house. And there was no sign of Benjamin.

"What's going on?"

Charles' brother Douglas had been living in the guesthouse ever since his wife threw him out ten months ago. He came up on the porch.

"I was about to come over for some breakfast when I heard you call. Why are you out here in this weather?"

Charles grunted. "It's Benjamin. He wasn't in his bed when his sister went in this morning to wake him up."

"Oh, really?"

Charles sighed.

"And now you think he's with her, am I right?"

Charles nodded. "Maybe."

"I'll go with you," he said.

"You don't have to do that," Charles said. "I know how to deal with my own son."

"Oh, I know you do. If anyone does, it's you. Still, you might need an extra set of eyes in this weather. Not a lot of visibility right now."

Charles looked out at the snow, then up at the dark skies above. It was getting lighter out now, but the thick cover of clouds made it seem like the night would never end.

Before leaving, they went around the back and looked inside the shed; they peeked under the porch and walked through the backyard, calling his name to make sure he wasn't still there. When they came back, Beatrice and Penny were looking at them from the window, clinging onto each other, worried eyes lingering on the men.

Charles walked up to the door, then rushed inside, worry beginning to eat at him.

"Penny. When did you see him last?"

Penelope bit her lip. She barely looked at her father as she spoke. "Just before midnight. We were sitting in the living room, watching a movie when Savannah texted him and asked to talk to him out on the porch. He grabbed his jacket and went outside where they met. They had a fight and were talking loudly, sometimes yelling at each other."

Penelope looked up at her mother briefly, then continued.

"Before he went out on the porch, I reminded him to lock up when he came back inside."

"But he never came back inside," Charles said. "The door wasn't locked. He must have gone with her. That is the only reasonable explanation."

"His phone is still on the table inside," Penny said. "In the living room."

"Maybe he forgot it," Charles said.

"Let's go see if he is at her place," Doug said. The tip of his nose was turning red in the cold or maybe it was from drinking the night before. It seemed to Charles that his brother's nose was always a little red.

"Let's go fetch that unruly son of yours at his girlfriend's place."

Doug put his hands in his pockets to hide how badly they were shaking.

Charles wrinkled his nose as they approached the garage. "Don't call her that, please."

Doug shrugged. "I know you don't like her, but it's what she is, and the more you don't approve of her, the more you're pushing him into her arms; you do realize that, right? Just because he's the son of a preacher doesn't mean he's not going to get himself in trouble. He's a boy. It's what they do. Don't you remember your own teenage years, huh? Or do I need to remind you?"

"Let's just go, shall we? And no talking, please," he said as the engine of his pick-up roared to life, while he wondered if he had heard a tremor in his daughter's voice when she spoke, or it was just his imagination. It sounded very similar to all the times when she had covered for her brother earlier in life.

Savannah Kelsey lived half a mile away. Her mother owned and ran Smoky Mountain Trailer Park, a campground for tourists located in downtown Maggie Valley, and they lived in a camper on the property. Savannah and her mother were new in town and had only arrived two years ago when they bought the campground using the money that they had received from selling their house back in Newark after Savannah's dad had died from lung cancer.

Charles parked the car in front of their trailer, then ran out through the intense snow and wind toward their door and knocked, his brother coming up behind him, covering his face from the snow with the hoodie of his jacket. A second later, the knocking turned to pounding before a light was turned on in one of the windows and Charles could hear movement inside. The door was opened, and a woman looked at him.

"Charles?"

Charles looked into her eyes, then swallowed. "I'm sorry to wake you up, Susan, but I need to talk to Savannah, please."

"Savannah? Why?"

"I'm sorry, Susan. I wouldn't be here if it wasn't important. Can we come in?"

Susan Kelsey stared at him, then at his brother. She lifted her nose slightly. "I'd rather you stayed outside. What is this about?"

"It's about Benjamin," Charles said, finally able to get the words through his lips. "We need him to come home with us."

Susan looked at him, then tilted her head. "He's not here if that's what you think. You know I would never let him spend the night here. My daughter is seventeen; I am not letting some boy ruin her."

Charles swallowed. That was what he feared she might say. He knew Susan wouldn't let Benjamin spend the night, but he had hoped she might have changed her mind with the heavy snowfall and the danger of the boy hurting himself when driving home.

"Can we talk to Savannah, then? We'd like to ask her if she knows where he might be."

Susan sighed. "I'm not sure why I would let you."

"Please," Charles said, clenching his fist in restraint. "It'll be just for a minute."

Susan watched him, scrutinized him, then let her shoulders come down. "All right. One minute then. I can have her come to the door."

He nodded, barely looking at the woman in front of him. "Okay. Do that. Please."

She left, and they could hear murmuring from the back of the trailer, then more voices, and soon Susan reappeared, followed by Savannah. She was a beauty and Charles couldn't deny that he understood why his son had fallen for the girl.

"'What's going on?" Savannah asked, sleep still in her eyes.

"We're looking for Benjamin. He talked to you last night on our porch, and we haven't seen him since. He's not answering his phone. Could you please tell me where he might be?"

Savannah blinked those gorgeous blue eyes behind the brown curls. Charles wrinkled his forehead and looked briefly at her mother standing behind her, then back at the girl.

"Please."

"I...I haven't seen him since last night. I left him outside on your porch."

"So...he didn't go with you?" Charles asked. "Because he never walked back inside the house."

Savannah shook her head. "No. We...the thing is, I broke up with him and then I left. Last time I saw him, he was standing on the porch looking after me as I backed out of the driveway. I remember looking at the clock in the car; it was 11:50."

"So...so you don't know where he is?" Charles asked again even though he had heard her the first time. "And you left him there. After breaking up with him, you left him standing there in his most fragile state of mind?"

As the flood of thoughts tore through his mind, Charles grew worried and suddenly restless. Panic was spreading through his body like cancer, and it refused to let him go. As Charles stared at the young girl in front of him, he could hear nothing but the tormenting sound of his own heartbeat. In his pocket, his phone buzzed, and he grabbed it and saw a text from his wife asking:

HAVE YOU FOUND HIM?

Charles stared at the display, the phone shaking in his hand, then put it back in his pocket and looked at his brother.

"Let's keep looking. He's got to be here somewhere."

PART I

THREE WEEKS LATER

1

The key was smeared in blood as she turned it in the ignition. Eliza Reuben felt the stickiness between her fingers and tried to rub it off on a towel she had in the car for the dog to lie on when she was wet from running in the snow after their long walks. But the blood wouldn't come off, no matter how much she rubbed. Eliza whimpered, then decided it had to wait. She had no time to waste. She threw the bloody towel on the floor, then backed out of the driveway and drove into the street, looking frantically in her mirrors.

She turned the car onto the big road, then hit the accelerator and rushed out of the neighborhood. She muttered little prayers under her breath while she drove down the street, looking into the rearview mirror, the sticky blood smearing her steering wheel.

Flashes of the dead body with those blank staring eyes, the pool of blood on the floor beneath him, kept blinking in front of her eyes. She was gasping for breath as she kept seeing the body bounce underneath her hands, while her own screams echoed off the walls.

As Eliza hit Soco Road, she turned the wheel, and the car skidded sideways on the icy road and ended up in the snow. She shrieked and managed to get the car back onto the asphalt, then floored the pedal once again and the car jolted forward. As she did, a car came up behind her, the driver honking his horn as it barely avoided smashing into her.

Eliza's heart hammered against her ribs as she watched the car pass her, followed by a big truck that also honked at her.

You've got to get out of here. You've got to get away.

Eliza floored the accelerator once again, and the car jumped forward at full speed. As she moved forward again, she glanced at the passenger seat next to her, which held her laptop. Heart pounding in her chest, she wondered about her old mother, about her alcoholic brother, and especially about Paige, her beloved golden retriever. Who was going to take care of all of them when she was gone? How would they get by? Her mother needed her to grocery shop for her and would miss her at their Sunday night dinners. Where would her brother crash when he got too drunk to drive home? Would he drive anyway and kill himself? Or maybe run into some nice family on their way home and destroy their lives just like his had been destroyed when a motorcyclist had run into his pregnant wife and killed her on the spot? And Paige? Who was going to take her running in the mountains in the spring? Who would make sure she got her medicine? Her mother couldn't take care of a dog, and neither could her brother, who could be gone for days on one of his benders. She would end up in some shelter, wouldn't she? Would they know how to take care of her? Was she too old to be rescued? Or would they have to put her down?

Eliza felt like crying at the thought as her eyes left the laptop and she glanced back at the road. She slammed her hand into the steering wheel a couple of times, yelling into the empty car when she glanced in the rearview mirror once again and spotted the truck behind her.

Then her heart dropped.

The truck was pushing closer and came up right behind her. The engine roared, and the truck ran into the back of her car, bumping it lightly. Not enough to leave a dent or a mark, but enough to let Eliza know this driver meant business.

Eliza gasped and stared at the truck in the mirror, then down at the laptop next to her, knowing its content was what the driver was after and she'd have to make sure they didn't get ahold of it.

Even if it cost her everything.

2

"**H**ead, *shoulders, knees, and toes, knees and toes. Head, shoulders, knees, and toes, eyes, ears, mouth, and nose."*
I looked in the rearview mirror at my kids while singing. Tyler was screaming the words out while touching his body parts.

"Could we please just stop singing that stupid song?" Abigail complained from the furthest back seat, where she sat with her twin brother, Austin, and their stepsister, Angela. Together, the three of them were also known as the three A's. Meanwhile, our adopted daughter, Betsy Sue, was sitting right behind me, earbuds in her ears, probably listening to a song by my wife—and her adoptive mother— the famous country singer, Shannon King. Next to her, we had made room for her imaginary ghost friend, Billy, who was still with us even though Betsy Sue was now eleven years old. Next to Billy sat our youngest son, Tyler, strapped into his car seat. The car was a Cadillac Escalade that I had bought just a month ago, realizing we didn't have enough room in my Jeep or Shannon's minivan for all of us if we wanted to go on a trip like this. The Escalade was an eight-seater, so there was plenty of room for all of us, including any imaginary friends. We had left Emily at home since she was busy applying for colleges and reading all my books on criminology so she could get ahead of her future classmates. She had decided to become a detective like her dad, and nothing in this world could make me prouder. It was a decision she had made while we were on a trip to the Bahamas a few months earlier, where she had also decided to finally begin the fight against her anorexia. She had started counseling and was taking her recovery very seriously, enough for us to feel safe enough to leave her alone while we took all the kids skiing in North Carolina for the first time in their lives. We had asked Emily to come too, but she was the one who had told us she preferred to stay home and take care of our dog.

"What? You don't like the song?" I asked, surprised. "You used to love singing this song."

"Well, now I think it's stupid," Abigail said. "Plus, it's kind of hard to do the movements properly when you're sitting down."

Shannon gave me a look and smiled. "The girl has got a point. Plus, we have actually sung it like twenty times now. I hate to say it, but it's getting a little old."

"Aw, but I love this song," I said.

"Me too, Daddy," Tyler yelled. "I love it too!"

I looked at my three-year-old, who was chewing on his pacifier that we ought to have taken from him a long time ago but didn't have the heart to yet. He wasn't allowed to use it in his preschool, so it was only when he was sleeping or driving in the car and we needed him to remain calm. So far, he had napped for two hours of our nine-hour drive.

Shannon yawned and looked at the clock, then up at me. She reached out her hand and grabbed mine in hers, then held it tight.

"I am so glad we're doing this. It's going to be wonderful to feel the snow again and just to be us, just be a family."

"I'm not going to argue against that," I said.

Things had been awesome between Shannon and me lately. She had been off the pills for six months now and seemed to be doing better than ever. She had taken the entire year off from touring and concerts and had been writing music in her studio at our house instead, something that left her with great joy. More than once, she had told me that she now remembered why she had originally started a career in music. She simply loved creating songs and having this outlet for her emotions. I just enjoyed having her at home every day and had been working from home a lot lately as well, being privileged to have a boss at CBPD who let me do so. That way, we could have lunch together on most days, and I enjoyed it immensely when seeing her happy face as she came out of her studio after hours in there, her cheeks rosy red and her eyes glistening with glee.

"This is what I was meant to do," she would often say when we enjoyed our coffee on the porch of our beach house in the afternoon right before the kids came home from school and the house was once again turned into an inferno of screams and obligations. "This is what I truly love to do."

It was great to see her so happy, but I knew she also loved standing on the stage. I knew that was a big part of her too. Even though she didn't say so, she missed it. She loved to share the songs with her audience, and I knew I couldn't keep her for myself for very much longer, but so far, I had enjoyed every moment I got.

It was my idea to go on this trip and teach the kids how to ski. Shannon had been skiing all her life, and so had her daughter, Angela, whereas I had only been snowboarding when I was younger. It was a couple of years now—or if I was honest, at least fifteen—since I had been to the mountains last, but I figured I could still remember how to snowboard. It was hardly something you forgot how to do, right?

I sure hoped not.

3

S hannon gleamed at Jack, then exhaled. In the back, the three A's were debating something very loudly about an Anime character, and it was about to turn into a fight, she could sense from the tone that was being used. Tyler was still singing the song and touching his head and shoulders and toes, but he was the only one still going at it.

Shannon felt such a deep sense of belonging that she had never felt before. It had been going on for quite some time now, ever since she had told her record label that she was taking a break and devoting herself completely to her family. They were naturally on her case about it and kept contacting her agent to ask if she was ready to get back in the game soon, bringing her offers that were hard to turn down. But so far, she had turned them all down. She needed this break. Living a normal life of packing lunchboxes and doing laundry and kissing scraped knees wasn't something Shannon enjoyed much, not the way Jack did. With six children in the house, there was always something or someone to attend to, and sometimes she missed the old life of touring and performing.

On the other hand, she enjoyed the calmness that had been over her life lately. It was very unlike anything she had ever felt in her tumultuous time here on earth. And Angela had never been happier either. She couldn't ignore that. The stability of having her mother close and of staying in one place and feeling the close-knit community surrounding them gave her exactly what she needed right now. And the way that Jack's parents had managed to take Angela in like she was their own made it a lot easier for Shannon to accept the fact that Jack's mother wasn't very fond of Shannon. Shannon knew his mother was just being protective of her son because of all that he had been through with his first wife, Austin and Abigail's mother, who ran out on them and was later killed. She didn't want her son to go through another heartbreak. But Shannon was trying so hard to get her mother-in-law to like her, and she hadn't come around yet. It tormented her slightly, especially since they were so close, living just a few houses down from them. Shannon was happy at the prospect of getting away for a week; she had to admit.

Shannon had suggested they could go to Vail or Lake Tahoe or somewhere bigger, maybe in Colorado, but Jack had told her that he knew of this small place in North Carolina. It was a place where the kids would learn really quickly because it was such a smaller area, and there were hardly any people who knew of it, so you'd meet mostly locals on the slopes. He used to go there with his buddies when he was in his twenties, and he loved the place. Shannon had been skeptical at first but then realized if she was to go anywhere and not be the center of attention, this could actually be it. In a small place, it was easier to stay incognito, and that was all she wanted right now. In Cocoa Beach, they had gotten used to her by now, and only tourists turned their heads or asked for autographs, which meant if she stayed away from the most touristy places, she could actually live a life as close to normal as possible. Every now and then, paparazzi would show up outside of her house and take pictures of her as she drove the kids to school, but it wasn't very often anymore. They left her alone these days for the most part.

"This is it. We're almost there now," she said as they drove off the highway and she could see the mountains towering in front of her. They were enveloped in a thick layer of fog, which she guessed had given them the name, the Great Smoky Mountains. They weren't as tall as the mountains Shannon was used to skiing in, but they were still gorgeous.

Jack glanced at her, and they smiled at one another, feeling excited about this adventure for their family. Shannon and Jack both wanted them all to enjoy skiing so they could do this every year and make it a family thing they did together. She had booked ski school for all the children, even though Angela didn't need it, but so she could be with the others. She was mostly nervous about Tyler, but he didn't seem to be afraid of anything, and Jack was certain he was going to do just fine.

"He has short legs. If he falls, he doesn't fall very far," he had said with a grin when they discussed it.

"Turn right here," Shannon said and pointed at the sign to Maggie Valley and the Cataloochee ski area.

Jack took the turn and soon they could spot the city limit sign ahead, telling them they were now entering Maggie Valley. The children had their noses glued to the windows.

"It's so cold," Austin exclaimed as he put his hand on the glass. "And look...there's snow on the sides of the road; look at all that snow!"

Shannon and Jack exchanged a look and smiled again. It was the first time the kids had seen snow, except for Angela. Tyler shrieked and pointed.

"And tomorrow, kiddos, you'll all be swooshing down those mountainsides up there," Jack said and pointed to where you could see the slopes.

"Wow," Abigail said. "I can't wait! I've never tried skiing before, so I'm pretty sure I'm good at it."

Shannon chuckled, then looked at the three A's in the backseat. Austin looked excited until he saw the slopes on the mountainsides.

"We're going up there?" he asked, his voice trembling slightly. "All the way up there?"

"Yes," Jack said as they passed the sign and entered the small town. "It's gonna be so much fun. You just wait and see. By the end of the week, you're gonna be shooting down the black slope with your daddy. You'll see."

Shannon glanced at the boy in the back, then saw how he sunk into his seat. Jack didn't notice it, but she did. The boy was terrified by the thought of having to ski. But worse than that, he was also afraid of disappointing his dad. It was the same with surfing. His twin sister was an excellent surfer like her dad, whereas Austin never really liked it. But Jack refused to see it and kept telling him he'd get better if only he practiced more.

They drove past a few restaurants, then a trailer park and some cabins next to a souvenir store with a huge bear figure on display.

"Isn't it quaint?" Jack said and looked out the windshield. "I love this place. It brings back so many mem..."

Jack didn't get any further before something happened in front of them. On the road ahead, running in the opposite direction of their car, a small car was driving fast, speeding toward them, tires screeching, zigzagging dangerously close to the oncoming cars.

"What the heck...?" Jack asked and lifted the pressure on the accelerator. The car came closer still and was soon driving almost on their side of the road.

"Jack!" Shannon screamed, then reached over and pulled the wheel in his hand, turning the car away just as the oncoming car came so close it scratched against the side of theirs.

Jack yelled, Shannon screamed, and so did the kids as the car skidded sideways. In the brief seconds that the oncoming car scratched against theirs, Shannon locked eyes with the woman inside of it before it was gone again. Shannon closed her eyes when she heard the loud crash coming from behind them, and when she opened them again, the Escalade had come to a stop. Heart beating rapidly in her chest, she looked around to see if any of the children had been hurt.

"Is everyone okay?" she asked.

They all nodded that they were.

Shannon clasped her chest. "What a scare."

That was when she finally looked out the windshield at what Jack was staring at. In front of them, the car that had almost hit them had rammed into a storefront, and smoke was emerging from it.

4

"Call 911," I yelled and took off my seatbelt. I jumped out of the car while Shannon yelled something I didn't hear. I stormed toward the crashed car and spotted the driver inside, clamped between metal and the blown-up airbag. I tried to open the door, but it wouldn't budge, so I went to the passenger side and managed to pull that open instead. I peeked inside the cabin and spotted a woman. Her head was bleeding heavily, and there was glass everywhere. She wasn't stuck, so I carefully grabbed her arm and pulled her toward me, then managed to get a grip on her shoulders and soon pulled her completely out of the car and put her on the ground. Shannon came out from our car and rushed toward me.

"They're on their way," she said, panting and agitated. "Is she...is she still alive?"

"There's no pulse," I said and pressed on her chest, then blew air into her lungs. "But I am not losing her now. Not on my watch."

In the distance, I could hear sirens, and I lifted my head, then wiped my face and was smeared with the woman's sticky blood on my cheek. As I lifted my gaze, I spotted a black pick-up truck parked a few feet away. It was just sitting there, the motor humming like it was waiting for something. As I looked at it, trying to see who was inside, it suddenly took off and disappeared down the road before I could see the license plate.

"Shoot," I said and glared after it. The truck sped down the street and took a right turn, then was gone. "Did you see that truck?"

"What truck?" Shannon asked. "What are you talking about, Jack? There's no truck."

"There was one, and it was parked right over there before it took off when it realized I was looking at it," I said and shook my head. I knelt next to the woman before I continued performing CPR, placing my hands on her bloody chest, then pressing rhythmically, while praying under my breath asking God for the strength and ability to be able to keep her alive long enough for the ambulance to arrive.

"Please, don't let her die, God. Please, help me keep her alive."

A few minutes later, the area was crawling with uniforms. Paramedics took over and rushed the woman into an ambulance, while I gave a deputy from the sheriff's office my statement of what I had seen, which frankly wasn't much. Then I gave him all my contact information and told him where we were staying in case they needed me.

"Probably won't be necessary. It seems like a terrible accident," Deputy Winston said and closed his notebook. "She must have been speeding and lost control of her vehicle."

"She was definitely going too fast," I said.

"Well, you're a lucky man, Detective Ryder. One inch closer, and she would have taken you all down with her."

I turned around and looked at my car with all the children in it as the realization sunk in. The deputy was right. If Shannon hadn't pulled the wheel when she did, we would have all been in ambulances by now.

Shannon stood next to me, her hands shaking from both cold and shock. I grabbed her hand in mine and smiled gratefully.

"You have no idea."

5

---

aggie Valley 2017

She had only been in town for a total of three weeks when Savannah Kelsey met Benjamin Rutherford. She already knew who he was since she—like most people in Maggie Valley—went to his father's church, and there he was usually sitting in the first row looking dashing. Savannah noticed him on the first Sunday they attended the church, but he didn't see her, and it took a few weeks before she finally got to talk to him. It happened in front of Joey's Pancake House on Soco Road, the town's main street on a Saturday morning. He was hanging out by his brother's pick-up truck, leaned up against it, chatting with two girls, of whom Savannah only knew one. Her name was Leslie, and she sat next to Savannah in their third-period science class at the high school.

"Hi, Savannah," Leslie said as Savannah passed them, trying not to look at the boy. She was going to pick up two omelets and bring them home for her and her mother to eat. Buying the campground had turned out to be a lot of work, and her mother barely had time to stop and eat between chores.

It had been one of her mother's crazy ideas. When Savannah's dad died after being sick with cancer for three whole months, her mother had sat in the living room crying for three days. Suddenly, she had walked into Savannah's room in their house in Newark and told her they were leaving. She was sick of feeling sorry for herself, and she had to get away. She had seen an ad online for a campground that was for sale in North Carolina, and she wanted to buy it. A few weeks later, the sale went through, and they packed everything and moved. Savannah was naturally devastated to have to leave her friends, but she was also grieving the loss of her father and was sick of being the girl who lost her dad at the school. She couldn't stand the way people treated her like they were afraid she might break down every moment or gasping when they accidentally mentioned her father or just the word *dad* like Savannah was unable to stand hearing the term. But it wasn't just the sympathy stares or the tilting of heads as she spoke to people that made her want to leave. It was just as much the fact that she felt so guilty inside. Because she wasn't sad that her dad died. She was sad that he wasn't there anymore, yes. She was devastated that he would never see her graduate or get married, yes, but she was happy that he had finally found peace, that he was free from all the pain he had been in. And it was so hard to explain to people that his death came as a relief to the people who loved him. People wouldn't understand till they had actually seen a loved one in that type of pain or going through months of watching them waste away, seeing the anxiety and panic in their eyes grow every day. That was the hard part. It was the screaming at night when the painkillers stopped working, or the panic when he couldn't breathe, or the fear that he would die when his wife was in the bathroom. Those were the tough things to deal with. Not the part when he actually passed away. That was the merciful part; that was the relief. Savannah struggled to explain that to her friends, especially because it filled her with overwhelming guilt. Coming to a new place, starting over, was just what they both needed.

"Have you met Benjamin Rutherford?" Leslie asked.

Savannah felt herself blush even though she tried to fight it as his green eyes landed on her. Benjamin Rutherford wasn't tall; that would be a lie to say. He was barely taller than Savannah, and she was short even for a girl. His shoulders were broad and almost made up for his lack in height, Savannah believed. And what he didn't have there, he held in his smile and sparkling eyes, full lips, and blond hair that reached his ears and sometimes fell into his eyes before it was brushed away with a swift movement.

"This is Savannah," Leslie said addressed to him. "You might have seen her around school. She's new in town."

"Nice to meet you," Benjamin said with a smirk. He reached out his hand, and she briefly touched it before she turned away.

"Anyway, I have to pick up some food," she said, rushing away so he wouldn't see her flushed face. She shivered lightly as she felt his eyes on her. It was late summer in North Carolina, but it didn't seem to get very warm in the mountains.

"Do you bike? A bunch of us are going biking in the mountains this weekend," Benjamin suddenly said as she had made it a few steps away. "Maybe you'd want to go with us?"

Savannah stopped. She stood for a few seconds and thought it over, then turned around and looked into his glistening eyes.

"I don't have a bike."

"Sure, you do. My brother doesn't use his anymore," he said. "You can have it if you like."

Savannah lifted herself on her tippy toes for a second, then smiled shyly. "I won't take it to keep, but if I could borrow it, then that would be fine, and I would love to go."

6

It was a lot later than expected that we arrived at the cabin that I had rented. It was dark out and way past Tyler's bedtime when we drove up the long driveway and got out.

I took a deep breath of the fresh mountain air, then shivered in the cold. It had recently snowed, and everything was covered in white powder. The children all gasped happily when they set their feet in it and heard the creaking sound it made under their feet. Abigail bent down, gathered a handful of snow, and threw the ball at her brother. She hit him on the shoulder, and Austin complained. A second later, they were both in the pile of snow next to the car, fighting and laughing.

Tyler had fallen asleep in his seat while we finished talking to the local police, and Shannon took him in her arms, ready to carry him inside the cabin. I found the key in the mailbox as the owner had promised me it would be, and unlocked the door, then turned on the lights.

"It's gorgeous," Shannon whispered as she walked past me, and I held the door for her. "I love the thick wooden beams."

It was perfect, just the way I had hoped it would be. Thick, heavy wood was everywhere, along with a beautiful stone fireplace and a strange bear figure standing by the door. I was just sad my family didn't get to arrive while it was still light out and they could see the creek in the backyard. But at least we could still hear it.

"I'm gonna find a bedroom for him upstairs," Shannon said and kissed my cheek.

"It's supposed to have five bedrooms, so you can choose any of them. I expect the three A's to sleep together while Betsy Sue will probably want her own room away from the younger kids."

I smiled at Betsy Sue as she walked past us, holding her backpack in her hand. She had grown so much the past year that she was almost unrecognizable. She was two years older than the three A's, and I knew that was important at that age. She felt more like one of the adults than one of the kids, and she hung out more with Emily back at the house than she did with the kids. Turning eleven had changed her, and she was going to be a teenager soon, even though there were still times when her childish innocence came forth, mostly due to the fact that she lived the first ten years of her life trapped inside of a house she wasn't allowed to leave. Her skin had gotten used to the sunlight by now, and she was over the shock of coming into the real world with everything it contained, but there was still so much that was new to her...like snow and like having a family. She kept mostly to herself, and I often tried to engage her in the family more and have her join us when we played board games, but she usually wasn't very interested. For the most part, she just wanted to listen to music and read books. We still played Black Jack every now and then, just the two of us, and that was the way I could get her to socialize a little, which I felt was important for her. She hadn't made any friends in school as far as we knew, and it worried me.

"They think I'm weird," she would say if I asked her about it. "They don't want to be friends with me. But that's okay. I don't really need friends. I have Billy."

Billy was the ghost with the yellow skin that she had brought with her from Savannah when we found her. He had died from yellow fever and, apparently, he was her best friend and had been since she was a child. I was hoping he would go away soon and that she would hang out with real living friends, but so far, it hadn't happened. I was worried that the fact that she still had an imaginary friend was one of the reasons why she wasn't making any real friends, but Shannon had told me to relax. Betsy Sue would get friends when she was ready for it, and Billy would become less important over the years.

"It's not something you can force away," she had said and kissed my forehead lovingly. "I used to have an imaginary friend too."

"How long did he stay with you?"

"Who says he ever left?" she said with a glint in her eye.

As I watched them all carry their suitcases and bags up the stairs, Abigail dragging hers, so it bumped on each step, I chuckled to myself. Once more, I sent a grateful glance toward the sky, thanking my guardian angels for keeping us safe today. Then I turned around and walked back to the car to carry the remaining few suitcases inside. As I opened the back hatch and grabbed two of them, I turned and stared at the house next door. There was a small light in the top window, and it looked like someone was sitting there, looking out...a dark figure rocking back and forth in a chair.

Shannon came back outside and stood next to me. I could see her breath in the porch light when she spoke.

"Tyler is down for the night, and the rest are on their way to bed too. I told them to get ready right now, even though Abigail complained loudly. I want them to be rested for tomorrow when we're going skiing. What's wrong?"

I shook my head. "Nothing. I just...there's someone in the window up there."

Shannon glanced toward the neighboring house. "You're right. There is someone sitting up there in the tower window. That is a little creepy. Let's hurry up and get inside, shall we? It's below freezing out here. My skin is hurting from the cold."

I shrugged and closed the back of the car. It blinked and lowered slowly. I grabbed two suitcases while Shannon took the last one. We walked inside and put them down, then closed the door behind us just as it started to snow again. Shannon and I put the kids to bed, then laid under the covers in our own bed, cuddling. I closed my eyes and held her tightly in my arms, wondering how I got so lucky to have all this.

Shannon shivered.

"Are you cold?" I asked.

She shook her head. I looked into her eyes.

"You're thinking about what happened today, aren't you?"

She nodded. "How can I not? It was so close, too close for my comfort. It was scary. Do you think she'll survive?"

I exhaled and rubbed Shannon's arm. I hadn't been able to get it out of my mind either. I didn't want it to ruin our family vacation, so I tried to not think about it, but it was hard not to.

"I hope so. I think I'll call the sheriff tomorrow and check if they have any news."

"I'd like that," she said and shivered again. I pulled her closer. "It's just...I looked into her eyes, Jack. Right before she crashed, I looked straight into her eyes. And I can't help thinking she looked scared, Jack. She looked terrified, and there was nothing I could do to help her. I keep seeing that face and those eyes again and again and wondering what went through her mind in that instant."

"Probably not a whole lot," I said and kissed her. "Now, let's get some sleep, okay? Big day tomorrow. We need our rest too."

7

Tyler woke us up early. He came storming into our room and threw himself on top of us, then giggled. I blinked my eyes, then moaned tiredly. It was barely light outside yet.

"It's too early, Tyler," I moaned.

The boy chewed his pacifier and glared at me like he had no idea what I was talking about. Then I chuckled, leaned over him, and lifted my hands in the air.

"Early bird gets the tickle monster," I said.

Tyler shrieked joyfully, and I tickled him till he begged me to stop, then he jumped down and ran out of the room. I was sitting up now and turned to look at my wife next to me. Then I snuggled up behind her and kissed her neck. She moaned and kissed me back. I put my hand on her breast.

"You do realize we're on a family vacation, right?" she asked and looked deep into my eyes. "As in...we have children everywhere, hearing us."

I groaned. "So, nothing for the entire week?"

She shook her head, then regretted it. "You think the walls are soundproof?"

"I'm positive they are," I said and hammered on it. "They won't be able to hear a thing."

She laughed. "Okay. If you say so."

"So tonight? When they're all asleep?"

She kissed me again. "It's a date."

We stayed in bed for about fifteen minutes more, just cuddling and talking, then got dressed in our ski clothes and walked downstairs where all the kids were hanging out. Tyler had found a box of Duplo Legos and emptied it on the floor, and now he was building something.

"Dad, we're starving," Abigail said without even looking up at me.

"But are you dressed?" I asked. "For skiing?"

They all looked at one another.

"We don't know how to," Austin said.

"I'll show you," Shannon said. "Come with me. All of you. You too, Tyler."

Tyler whined, annoyed because he had to leave his Legos. He looked at me like I could save him. I shook my head and signaled for him to listen to his mother, and so he went. I walked to the living room and turned off the TV, then knelt on the floor to pick up the Legos. I glanced out the window and saw the creek, then opened the door and walked out on the porch to feel the cold air on my face. As I stared at the rippling water, I couldn't help but look toward the neighboring house. There was still someone sitting in the window, rocking back and forth, and now that it was daylight, I could see that it was a woman. She seemed to be in the exact same spot as the night before.

"Hello there!" a voice said coming up behind me. "You must be Jack Ryder and family."

I turned and spotted a small woman with her gray hair in a ponytail. Her smile was sincere and exited.

"Just Jack Ryder," I said. "The family's inside."

"I'm Bridget Westwood. Welcome."

I smiled when I recognized her name from the emails I had received with information on the cabin and where to find the key.

"Thank you," I said, still unable to keep my eyes off the woman in the window. Bridget saw it.

"She's waiting for her son to come home," she said with an exhale. "He's been gone for three weeks. No one knows where he is. It's been upsetting to the entire town. Beatrice has been sitting up there ever since the day he disappeared. I guess she wants to be the first to see him if he shows up. They fear that he might have drowned himself in Jonathan's Creek. I guess she watches to see if he turns up."

"Her son has been gone for three weeks?" I asked. "That's awful. How old is he?"

"He's seventeen."

"Ah. I see. Could he have run away with a girl?" I asked.

"Sure, except the girl is still in town living right down at the campground. Her mom runs the place, and she hasn't seen him since that same day either. Lots of people think she knows more than she's saying, though."

"What do you mean?" I asked.

"She was the last person to see him alive. Some say they believe she killed him. Others that she drove him to suicide. She broke up with him on that night."

"Why would she kill him if she broke up with him?"

"Maybe he broke up with her first; who knows?" she asked. "Maybe he screwed up and made her mad. It happens."

"Still fairly rare that a girl kills her boyfriend," I said. "It's usually the other way around. Besides, no one knows if he's dead, right? He could have just run away. Did he have trouble at home?"

"The pastor's son? No. He was spoiled rotten by those parents. They have three children, yet they loved Benjamin the most. Especially the mother. She'd do anything for him, jump at his every wink. Even his dear sister adores him."

"And the third child? Does he love him too?" I asked.

"He's a little trickier, Charles Junior. No one ever liked him much, not like they love his brother. He's always been a little to a side. He was a teenager when they moved here, practically an adult. An angry type, not very friendly like the two others who would always meet me with a smile or wave and say hallo. A shame what happened to him, though. Ended up in a wheelchair after some accident."

"That sounds terrible," I said, wanting to end the conversation there. I was never very comfortable around gossip and rumors. I had a feeling Bridget might be the center of information around this town. Every small town had one person who made sure everyone else was up to date on the latest, even if it was just speculations.

"Sure was." Her eyes settled on my clothes. "So, you and your family are going skiing today?"

"We hope to, yes. They're all in there, getting dressed."

"You couldn't have picked a better time to come. It's been snowing for days now, and the slopes should be perfect."

"Say, do you know where we could get a good breakfast around here? We need to get some solid food in us before we get there."

Bridget smiled. "I most certainly do. Joey's Pancake house on Soco Road. That's our main street that goes through the entire town; you drove it when you got here because it's the only way in and out. If you go right on it and continue, then just before you turn to go up the mountain, there's the pancake house. Best pancakes you'll ever get. I know because I work there as a hostess."

8

Shannon sighed with satisfaction and looked at all the kids in the back. It wasn't easy, but she had managed to get them all ready, and now they were finally on the road heading for a breakfast place. She wasn't that hungry but looked forward to a cup of coffee and a break. Getting five kids ready for skiing had turned out to be quite the challenge, especially Tyler, who had complained about the many layers of clothes she wanted him to wear.

"I'm not cold," he kept saying.

"You will be," she argued.

"I won't. I'm never cold."

"That's because you live in Florida. This isn't Florida; this is the mountains, and there is snow. You want to play in the snow, right?"

The discussion had continued well beyond what Shannon had patience for, but finally, the boy had given in and put on the layers. Now, he was complaining again that he was too hot in the car.

This is going to be a long week.

Jack was on the phone as they drove down the main street and Shannon looked out at this small town surrounded by mountaintops with its many restaurants and souvenir shops. It also had a big campground and a couple of small hotels and cabin rentals for the tourists who came to ski or hike in the mountains.

"What do you mean the sheriff isn't in right now?" Jack said angrily. "It's nine-thirty? How about Deputy Winston, is he in yet? Ah, I see. No, you can't take a message. Thank you."

He hung up and grumbled.

"So, no news?" Shannon asked. She felt terrible for the poor woman in that car the day before and couldn't stop wondering about her. Was she still alive?

"Apparently, the sheriff doesn't come in till later," Jack said with a snort.

"Wasn't there someone else you could talk to? How about that deputy that we talked to?" she asked.

"Not there either."

"Well, maybe they're out patrolling or something," she said as Jack left the main road and turned into a parking lot that was packed with cars. He found a small spot at the end of the lot.

"Joey's Pancake House," Jack said and killed the engine. "Supposed to be the best pancakes we've ever tasted. Are you ready for the best pancakes of your life, kids?"

They didn't even look up from their phones to answer. Only Tyler glanced at him, but he was so enveloped in his own anger that he had no time to cheer. Jack sent Shannon a look and a shrug.

"Let's just eat," she said and got out. She grabbed Tyler in her arms, and he struggled to get away from her, so she put him down but kept his hand in hers, tightly gripped. Ever since he was kidnapped back in Savannah, she had kept an extra eye on him constantly when going places. The fear still lingered beneath her skin.

Inside, they were greeted by a woman who seemed to know Jack. Her face lit up, and she put the menus under her arm before she announced, "Jack Ryder and family. Welcome."

"Thanks, Bridget," Jack said. "A table for seven?"

Betsy Sue cleared her throat and looked at Shannon for help.

"Don't forget Billy," she said while Tyler pulled her arm to get to a big bear statue standing in the corner next to an old map of the area.

Jack gave her a look. "I can't keep setting up an extra seat for him everywhere we go."

Shannon tilted her head, her eyes pleading. Jack glanced at Betsy Sue, then sighed.

Bridget looked from one to the other, then down at the girl, her face lighting up in a big smile.

"We have a perfect table for eight down in the corner," she said and winked at the girl.

"Thank you," Jack said. "That would be perfect."

Bridget showed them to their table, and as soon as they stepped closer, Shannon realized why it hadn't been possible for Jack to reach anyone at the sheriff's office. At a huge table next to where Bridget seated them sat a handful of men all in the same uniform.

9

"It's usually a good sign when the police eat here," Shannon said and sat down, placing Tyler next to her. "That's what my mom always told me."

The kids each found a seat, even Billy, and I was about to sit down too when Deputy Winston spotted me from his seat.

"Hey there," he said. "Ryder, right?"

"I should go say hello," I said to Shannon.

She nodded in agreement.

I walked over and shook hands with Deputy Winston. "This is Detective Ryder that I told you about. The guy from the crash yesterday."

The others nodded. A heavy guy, probably twice my size and a little older than the rest, reached out his hand.

"Nice to meet you, Detective. I'm Sheriff Franklin. Winston tells me you're from Florida?"

"Cocoa Beach Police Department. Used to work at the Brevard County Sheriff's Office but you know..." I said and glanced at my family.

"Too many kids to take care of?" The sheriff asked. "We know how that is. Beautiful family."

"Thanks. Listen...I actually called your office just a few minutes ago to ask about that woman...the one from the crash last night. Do you have any news about her? Did she make it?"

The sheriff cleared his throat. "She's still alive, but not conscious."

I breathed in relief. "But she'll survive?"

"They don't know yet," Winston said. "The crash caused a lot of damage to her brain, they say."

I nodded. "Okay. At least she's still alive. We've been so worried. That was a bad crash. I just hope she'll make it."

Sheriff Franklin chewed a piece of pancake and cleared his throat. "Not that it's any of your concern, but you might want to know that she was running away from the scene of a crime."

I wrinkled my forehead. "She was?"

"Murder," Winston said.

"Really?"

"We don't know the details yet, but she was seen leaving a house where we later found the body of a man, fatally shot in the chest. We found traces of his blood in the car that crashed and on the steering wheel. We took samples of the blood on her hands too and found the blood on hers was mixed with that of our dead man."

"We got one of them magic boxes," Winston said. "You know...the rapid DNA machines."

I knew what they were talking about and knew many police departments all over the country had gotten them within the past ten months. The magic box was a machine that provided results in ninety minutes, and the police could operate them themselves. It was called a revolution in DNA processing since we'd usually have to wait days for the same results from a lab. I was impressed that they had gotten one of these out here in the mountains when we were still waiting for ours at CBPD.

"So, you think she killed him?" I asked.

Sheriff Franklin finished chewing and sipped his coffee, slurping it. He seemed like a man who liked to take his time to think before he spoke.

He put his cup down, then got up and put his hat on, then tipped it. "We do. If she ever wakes up, we'll charge her as the first thing. It was nice to meet you, Detective. Enjoy skiing and your family."

10

Maggie Valley 2017

He took her to meet his family. For Savannah, that was a big step after only three dates, but Benjamin insisted that they wanted to meet her. He picked her up at the campground and drove her to his house, while she stared out the window, nervously fiddling with the edge of her shirt.

"Are you okay?" he asked.

Savannah nodded, biting her lip. "I'm fine."

It was a lie. She was everything but fine. She had no idea how his family would react when he brought home a girl like her. She wasn't exactly in his league. Benjamin was a pastor's son and his family was influential in this town; whereas Savannah was a poor girl who had no father and lived in a trailer park. They owned it, yes, but still. They had spent all they had on buying the campground and couldn't even afford a proper house for themselves.

Benjamin chuckled, then put his hand on her thigh. "They're going to love you. Don't worry. As soon as they realize how crazy I am about you, they'll welcome you with open arms."

Savannah forced a nervous smile, then looked out the windshield as they drove up to the house. She gasped when Benjamin stopped the truck in front of a beautiful old Queen Anne style house with decorated gables and a three-story tower anchoring the center, topped by a spire. As Benjamin held the door for her, Savannah got out, then felt like she was being watched and looked up at the double-story porch that extended across the front, where she spotted a figure standing there, looking down at them. In the distance, she could hear the rippling creek that went through most of the town and also through the Rutherford property. Benjamin had talked about it and how he and his sister would often go fishing during summer break and how he couldn't wait to take Savannah there as well. Savannah wasn't very fond of water, but she hadn't told him that.

"That's my sister," he said and waved at the girl standing up on the porch. "You're gonna love her."

Benjamin pulled her by the hand and onto the porch, while Savannah wondered if this was a good idea. She didn't have a comfortable feeling about it. Maybe she was just nervous.

"Mom, Dad? This is Savannah," Benjamin exclaimed as soon as he had dragged her through the door.

A tall and very blonde woman came down the stairs, walking with style and elegance, looking almost like she was floating lightly across the floor as she approached her. She had an air of arrogance, and the way she looked down at her made Savannah feel even smaller than she already was. The woman smiled, but it didn't seem friendly to Savannah. Not when it was combined with an elevator stare that made her regret having worn those ripped jeans that Benjamin had promised her wouldn't be a problem.

"So, this is Savannah. We've heard so much about you," his mother said and reached out a cold hand that Savannah shook with a nervous chuckle. She grew bewildered by her aloof tone.

"Nice to meet you, Mrs. Rutherford."

"I want you to meet Penelope," Benjamin said, then yelled up the stairs. "Penny! Come down here!"

He gave her a look of excitement while they waited, and

Savannah tried to hide just how awful she felt. Benjamin's mother's eyes were on her constantly, like she was studying her every feature to find out what her son could possibly like about her, wondering why he had dragged her home with him, why her of all the girls he could have chosen.

"PENNY!" Benjamin yelled, and his mother scolded him for yelling inside the house before she went into the kitchen. Penny still didn't show herself, but the dad did. He came out of his study, looking at his son, not even seeing Savannah.

"Benjamin, why are you yelling?"

"Dad, this is Savannah, the girl I've told you about."

The father forced a smile. "Hello, Savannah. Nice to meet you. Now, you two be quiet, please. I am working on my next sermon."

"It was nice to meet you, Pastor Rutherford," she said. "I enjoy your sermons very much."

The father grumbled something, that sounded like a thank you, then turned around and went back into his study. As Savannah turned around, someone was standing right behind her, and the shock made her jump.

"There you are!" Benjamin said as he turned around as well. "About time. Didn't you hear me call?"

The girl in front of them stared at Savannah up and down. She was a year and a half younger than them but looked to be about the same age. She was gorgeous and taller than Savannah, just like their mother, making her almost intimidating. Her straight blonde hair fell heavily on her shoulders, and her bright green eyes sparkled behind her bangs. Her skin was pale and her lips so ruby red they stood out in her face.

Savannah smiled. She had been looking forward to finally meeting Penny, whom Benjamin spoke about so much. She hoped that they could become friends so that she would have an ally in the house.

"Hi, Penny, I'm Savannah," she said and reached out her hand. She had thought about how to greet her while they drove there. She knew Penny was important to Benjamin, so she wanted to make a good impression on her more than anyone. But what was the best way to greet a boyfriend's sister for the first time? Did you hug her? Did you shake hands? In the car, she had decided that shaking hands was too formal, too grown up, yet there she was, holding out her hand for Penny to shake.

Penny stared at her hand, then looked up at Benjamin and smiled, almost beamed when their eyes met. She then threw herself into his arms in a warm embrace. He laughed and lifted her in the air, then spun around, while Penny's eerie glare met Savannah's and she felt her stomach churn.

11

"So, she was a fugitive?" Shannon asked.

I shrugged. We were sitting in the lift, being hauled up the mountain, the freezing air biting our cheeks. Beneath us, people were skiing the slopes, and my stomach fluttered at the thought of me being one of them in a few minutes. I couldn't wait. My snowboard dangled beneath me as I looked at Shannon.

We had dropped all the kids off at the ski school and signed the seemingly thousands of papers, then kissed each one of them and left. It had taken Shannon a few minutes before she was ready to leave Tyler, so we had stayed to watch them on the bunny slope for a little while to make sure he was all right. As we saw him wave and smile widely after his first ride down the small hill, we knew it was going to be okay and left. The instructors seemed nice and very competent. Now, I couldn't wait to snowboard with my love and have a little time for just the two of us doing something that we both loved.

"I guess so," I said. "It makes sense. It explains why she crashed and why she was speeding."

Shannon looked pensive as we were lifted higher and higher up.

"What's wrong?" I asked.

She shook her head. "It's nothing."

"Come on; I know you," I said. "I can tell you're thinking about something. You get that look on your face like you want to say something, but you're holding it back."

Shannon sighed. "Well...it's just that...I looked her in the eyes, Jack. I saw her right before she crashed, and all I saw was this...this intense, deep fear. She was scared, Jack. I can't stop thinking about how terrified she looked. I've never seen anything like it."

I nodded while looking down at a snowboarder who didn't seem to know how to stop and ended up sitting down, then sliding a few yards before he stopped.

"We don't know her motives or if she killed this guy or what was going on in her life," I said. "But I do know that if you're running away from the police, most people would be scared too. She had lost control of her car; that's pretty scary too."

Shannon exhaled. "It's just...I think it was more than that."

The lift ended at the top of the mountain, and we slid out of it, then glided down to the beginning of the black slope that the locals had named OMIGOSH. I put on my gloves and latched my helmet, then smiled at Shannon.

"This is our vacation," I said. "How about we let it go? The police are dealing with this, and there really isn't anything else we can do. Plus, we're here to enjoy ourselves, remember?"

She smiled and lifted her eyebrows. "Look who's talking. You're never able to let go."

That made me laugh.

"Touché. Race you to the bottom," I yelled.

I got myself ready to slide down the slope, then sent her a happy smile before tipping over the edge and riding down. As the cold air hit my face and I felt the joy lift me up, I still couldn't stop thinking about the truck I had seen drive away from the scene. What was it doing there and why was the driver in such a rush to get away when I spotted it? I hated to admit that Shannon was right, but something about this whole affair didn't feel good.

12

They picked up the kids to have lunch with them. Shannon felt exhausted—and a little sore—from hours of skiing, yet she couldn't stop smiling. It felt good to be back on the slopes again, and it was nice to have some alone time with Jack doing something they both loved. Even though Shannon got the feeling that Jack had been a little frustrated most of the morning, not quite able to make his snowboarding work. Shannon kept telling him it had been so many years that it was only natural that he needed extra time to get back into it. But proud as he was, he wouldn't admit it, even when he fell again and again and yelled angrily at the snow.

"I hate it."

The words came out of Austin's mouth as soon as he spotted his dad. Shannon grabbed Tyler in her arms and lifted him up. He was one big smile and had obviously enjoyed it. Angela and Betsy Sue seemed to have had a great time too, and Abigail said she loved every second of it.

"What do you mean, you hate it?" Jack asked, surprised. "You've been at it for three hours. You can't possibly know after that short of a time."

Austin looked at his father. "I do. I hate it. I hate the snow and how wet it is; I hate snowboarding; I hate falling; I hate the lifts. I hate everything about it, even the teachers except for Lyle; he's nice."

Jack sighed. Shannon felt a knot growing in her stomach. She knew how much Jack wanted his children to love snowboarding the same way he had always loved it and loved surfing. But he seemed to have forgotten—or ignored—the fact that Austin didn't enjoy surfing either. Austin wasn't the boy that Jack wanted him to be, and he kept falling short of his expectations. Austin enjoyed sitting inside and drawing or playing computer games, whereas Jack had always been the outdoorsy type who constantly wanted his son to come outside and skateboard or surf or climb trees. But that wasn't who Austin was, and in all the years Shannon had been with them, she had seen how he constantly failed to realize this. His twin sister, Abigail, was the tomboy. She enjoyed all that stuff that Jack did, but not Austin. And Shannon feared for the boy's self-worth if Jack kept this up. Would he end up thinking he wasn't enough for his dad if he constantly felt like a disappointment to him? Of course, he would.

Shannon hadn't wanted to meddle in how Jack raised the twins since he always got so defensive if she said anything, but she wasn't sure she could keep watching him do this to the boy over and over again. He was about to reach an age where he needed his dad's support more than ever.

"Nonsense, you just need to give it another try," Jack said and started to walk up the wooden stairs to the restaurant. Shannon followed, her heavy boots slamming hard into the surface of the steps.

"But I don't want to. I don't want to go back there ever," Austin said after him, but Jack was already up on the porch, and couldn't hear the boy, or maybe he was just pretending like he couldn't. Meanwhile, the girls all followed him closely, chatting and laughing, talking about how starving they were.

Shannon exhaled, then put Tyler down so he could walk the rest of the way on his own. She smiled at Austin, whose eyes had turned wet, then reached out and took his hand in hers.

"Let's get something to eat. Everything looks better on a full stomach, huh? I heard they have hot chocolate. I think hot chocolate is exactly what you and I need right now."

13

The figure in the long dark coat watched the children as they skied or snowboarded down the small slope, huge grins on their faces, some shouting with joy, others cheering loudly. It was the afternoon session, and they had just come back from their lunch break when the figure had arrived to watch. The figure stood at a distance among a small flock of parents who had been told they could watch, but not go beyond the fence. Some were clapping, others cheering loudly, but the figure didn't. The figure stood like it was frozen and simply observed.

Not all the children on the slope were happy, though. There was one kid, a boy, who kept sobbing and crying every time he fell. The figure watched as he was helped back up and then urged to try again. The boy cried and said he didn't want to, that he didn't like it. The teacher turned to another instructor for help, and they talked for a few seconds, then the first one told the boy that he could sit down for a few minutes, take a break, and then come back up with the others.

The figure's eyes followed the young instructor as he went back up the slope to the group of children and they started to descend one after another, sliding down the hill, some ending in falls, others lifting their arms in the air in excitement. Meanwhile, the boy from earlier unhinged his snowboard and walked to the side, dragging the board and throwing it in the snow, then sat down, sniffling.

The instructor let the others come down one after another, and they continued like that for about fifteen minutes before the instructor finally approached the boy again, kneeling next to him. The figure watched the two of them have a longer chat, and the boy kept shaking his head heavily and saying *no* so loud that everyone standing there could hear it. The instructor then looked up at the others and signaled that he would take the boy inside. His colleagues both gave him a thumbs-up, then focused on the other kids while the instructor helped the boy get up and they walked back inside the building housing the ski school.

The figure waited till they were inside before pulling down a ski mask to cover their face and then followed them.

14

————

"Are you thirsty? Do you want a juice box? I have some in the fridge over there."

Lyle looked at the young boy in front of him. He had red-rimmed eyes and tears were still streaming across his cheeks. He could barely breathe and kept gasping for air in agitation. Lyle felt for him; he really did. Some kids just didn't enjoy skiing or snowboarding, but that was often hard for the parents to accept if they loved it themselves.

Austin nodded between sobs.

"Okay, go sit over there," Lyle said and pointed at the bench. "I'll bring you one. Just give me a sec."

They were all alone in the room among the many skis and boots. The floors were wet, and it smelled like old sweaty socks. Lyle had decided to take the boy in there to offer him a little break and to be able to talk properly. In his years as a ski instructor, Lyle had seen this happen many times. The parents wanted their child to learn how to ski or snowboard, but the child didn't like it, yet felt like such a disappointment to his parents because he didn't. On top of it, Austin had his twin sister out there, and she was killing it. She was already so good that the other instructors had talked about taking her up on the mountain later in the day to ride her first green slope. It wasn't something they usually did until day two of ski school, but she was doing exceptionally well. Meanwhile, her brother hadn't even mastered the bunny slope yet. It had to be tough for a little guy like that.

Lyle walked to the mini fridge and took out a juice box, then handed it to Austin. He sat down in front of him and looked into his eyes while the boy drank.

"Listen, Austin. Snowboarding is fun, but it takes a while to learn. I'm sure if you try again, after getting a drink and maybe a snack, then you'll love it. Just don't expect to learn it in a day. I know falling makes it worse and you don't like that. But if you'll let me instruct you, I can take care of you and make sure you don't fall."

"I'll still fall," Austin said. "I always fall. I fall all the time. And it hurts, and I don't like it. I don't like being in this place and falling all the time. I just want to go home."

Lyle sighed. "Falling is kind of part of it. You can't snowboard without falling every now and then. But you learn how to get back up and continue and, in time, you'll fall less."

"So, what's the point?" Austin asked with a sniffle.

"The point is that it's fun when you're out there riding down those mountains. I know it doesn't seem like it right now, but I promise you, it's fun. It will be."

"Until you fall again," he said and shook his head.

Lyle smiled. "Yes. But then you get up and continue, and the more you do it, the less you fall. The most important thing is that you know how to stop. As soon as you know that, you can go anywhere on that thing. It'll be fun. Trust me."

Austin finished his juice box, then wiped his nose on his sleeve.

"What do you say, champ?" Lyle asked. "Are you ready to go back out there or do you need another minute?"

"Need another minute," Austin said and dangled his legs.

"Okay, we can do that. How about I find you a little snack? I bet you're starving. Snowboarding always makes me so hungry. How about some goldfish?"

Austin nodded, and Lyle went to the cabinet to open it. He grabbed a bag of goldfish, then turned to walk back to the boy when he heard the door slam shut and spotted a figure walk in.

"Excuse me?" he said. "This area is closed off right now. If you're looking for your child, they're all outside. All the kids are on the bunny slopes."

But the figure in the dark coat didn't stop to listen and soon walked into the back and faced Lyle. The figure was wearing a ski mask that covered their face, but Lyle could still recognize the eyes. They were boiling with anger and hatred.

"W-what are you doing here?" Lyle asked.

"You just couldn't keep quiet, could you?" the figure asked with a quivering voice. "You had to tell."

"I...I didn't...I'm sorry..."

"Yeah, well, it's too late for sorry," the figure said, then pulled out a gun with a gloved hand.

"Oh, hey, what are you doing?" Lyle asked and recoiled, holding his hands up in the air. "What are you doing with that thing? I have a child here."

The dark figure didn't seem to care. Instead, this figure reached over, grabbed Lyle's hand, and placed the gun in it. By force, the hand and gun were turned to face Lyle, squeezing his hand so hard it cracked.

"Please...don't..."

The figure leaned over and forced the gun in Lyle's hand toward his face. Lyle tried to fight back, to get the hand holding the gun out of the grip, but he wasn't strong enough, and soon he felt the cold steel as it was pressed against the bottom of his chin.

"Please...don't do this...I'll do anything. I'll take it back. I'll retract my statement and tell them I was lying, that it was all one big fat lie," Lyle begged, but as he looked into the eyes of the figure standing in front of him, pressing the gun and his hand, he realized it was no use.

It was too late.

The gun went off, and Lyle fell to the floor, limp as a rag-doll, blood spilling from the wound in his head. The figure then took Lyle's phone and tapped on the screen before returning it to Lyle's pocket. The dark figure glanced at Lyle, then turned and looked at Austin sitting on the bench, his pants soaked in pee.

The figure approached him, then bent down and looked him straight in the eyes. Loud voices were emerging from the outside along with the sound of boots moving fast across the pavement. The figure lifted a gloved finger to their lips, looked at the boy, and spoke right before slipping out the back door, saying: "Don't tell. Or I'll come after you next! I'll kill you and your entire family."

15

The day didn't turn out the way I wanted it to at all. I don't know what I had expected, but it wasn't what I got. I guess I had thought I would be able to remember how to snowboard and that I would soon be rocketing down the black slope like I used to when I was in my twenties. But for some reason, I couldn't get back into the rhythm of it, and I kept falling, while Shannon danced down the slope like it was the easiest thing in the world. I had thought it would help to get some lunch, that I just needed something to eat and a break, but as we had said goodbye to the kids again and got back up on the mountain, I quickly learned that it was going to take a lot more than that. I managed to get a third of the way down the steepest part of the black diamond—the same slope I used to be the king of—before I fell and started sliding down the icy slope. As I finally stopped sliding, when I was almost at the bottom, I sat up and groaned, annoyed. Shannon came down to me and stopped in front of me, spraying a huge blast of snow into the air.

"Are you okay? That was quite the fall. Did you hurt yourself?"

"I'm fine," I said without looking up at her. "I don't know what's wrong with me today."

"It's been fifteen years since you last went snowboarding, Jack. It's only natural. Don't be so hard on yourself. You're doing fine for someone who hasn't been snowboarding in fifteen years. What did you expect?"

"You haven't been skiing for a long time, and you don't seem to have any trouble," I said. "You're skiing like it's nobody's business, while I keep ending up in the snow."

"It's only been a few years for me," Shannon said. "I used to go every year with Angela before I moved to Cocoa Beach. You can't really compare us. It's hardly the same."

"Still, I surf. I should be able to do this. I hate that I keep falling."

She smiled.

"What?" I asked.

"Nothing. You just...you sound just like your son now."

I gave her a look. "You can be really annoying; do you know that?"

She nodded. "I do. But remember how you feel right now when we pick Austin up later today, okay? He needs you to understand him. That's all he wants from you. He was devastated at lunch because you didn't even want to listen to him."

"I listened to him. I heard every word he said. He was just whining, and I hate it when he does that," I said. "He has to learn that life is tough sometimes, and if you want something, you fight for it. He also needs to realize that whining will get you nowhere."

Shannon lifted her eyebrows at me, then said sarcastically: "And right now, you're the perfect example of that."

"Oh, come on," I said. "That's not fair."

"Really? To me, it seems exactly the same. Besides, had it been Abigail, then you'd have reacted completely different, am I wrong?"

I knew she was right but didn't want to admit it. It was just different when it was your son. I wanted him to like the same things as me; I wanted him to be strong and not give up because something was a little tough. But I had also seen the hurt in his eyes when I had brushed him off. I knew Shannon was right, but it still annoyed me that she meddled like that. I never said anything about how she raised Angela.

I exhaled, then gathered some snow and threw it at her. It hit her on the chest, and she laughed, then she used her pole to spray snow at me. I grabbed the pole and pulled her down with me, and she landed in the snow next to me. I stared her in the eyes, then kissed her.

Barely had our lips parted when my phone vibrated in my pocket. I took off my gloves and pulled it out.

"It's the ski school," I said and picked it up, my heart starting to beat faster. They had told us they'd only call in case of an emergency.

16

The police were already there when we got back down. I threw my snowboard in the snow, then ran as fast as I could in those stiff boots toward the building that housed the ski school. The blinking lights from the sheriff's police cruisers were reflected in the snow and lit the entire area up in an eerie blue glow that frightened me.

An instructor met me outside.

"What happened?" I asked. All they had told me on the phone was that there had been an accident involving a ski instructor and that my son was with him when it happened.

The instructor stared at me, her eyes blank in shock. "I...my colleague went inside...there was a loud blast and then Jim hurried in there and...found him."

"Found whom?" I asked. "Where is my son? Did anything happen to Austin?"

She shook her head. "He's fine, as far as I know."

"As far as you know? But...where is he now?"

"He's with the police, inside, but..."

I didn't stay to hear the rest of what she had to say. I rushed to the door and went inside, where a deputy stopped me.

"I'm sorry, sir. You can't go in there."

"My son is in there," I said. "I need to see my son."

"Ryder!" Deputy Winston came up to us, then addressed his colleague. "He's okay. You can let him in."

"Where is he?" I asked, bewildered. I took a few steps further inside the school area, saw the blood, and then the young man lying in the blood. I recognized him as one of the children's instructors.

"What happened?"

"We're trying to figure that out," Deputy Winston said. "Your son was there, and we're trying to find out exactly what happened. He's the only one who saw it."

"My son was? Austin? Is he okay?"

Winston nodded. "He's unharmed. But he won't say a word. Maybe you can get him to open up to us."

"He must be in shock. Can I see him? Can I see my son, please?"

"He's right over there," Winston said with a nod. He walked ahead of me, and I followed, heart pumping in my chest, a million thoughts rushing through my mind.

We found Austin sitting on a bench, Sheriff Franklin kneeling in front of him. He shook his head when he spotted us.

"Still won't say a darn thing."

"Austin!" I said and grabbed him in my arms. The boy hardly moved and felt stiff as a board. "Are you okay? Are you hurt?"

He looked into my eyes, then shook his head.

"He was at the other end of the room when it happened, sitting over there. That's where he was when we got here. And I don't think he moved at all."

Another deputy came up to the sheriff and whispered in his ear, then showed him a phone in a plastic bag.

Sheriff Franklin then turned to face us. "They say it looks like suicide. There's residue all over his hands and fingers. It looks like he shot himself. Plus, they found a series of texts he sent out right before it happened to his friends and family, saying *Sorry, I just couldn't take it anymore."*

"Suicide?" I asked, baffled. "Why on earth would anyone commit suicide in front of a little boy? Why even bring a gun to a ski school filled with children?"

Sheriff Franklin looked at the dead body that was now being covered up, then back at Austin.

"I don't know, to be honest. It does sound a little strange, but people who are depressed or suicidal don't really think rationally in my experience. They rarely think about anyone besides themselves. In my opinion, it's the most selfish thing you can ever do because you hurt so many people, especially the ones who love you, and you even sometimes ruin the lives of strangers. But that's just how I feel."

He glanced shortly at Austin as he said the last part, and I sensed that he felt bad for my boy. I sat next to my son, then looked down at him, fighting my tears, unable to fathom what could possibly force someone to do this to a little boy. I grabbed his hand in mine and realized it was still shaking.

17

Maggie Valley 2017

"She's ignored me all night."

"Nonsense," Benjamin said. "She's just shy."

Savannah looked around the restaurant in the direction of the restrooms. Penny hadn't come out yet. They were on a double date with Benjamin's sister and a guy she had recently started dating. But so far, Penny hadn't even given him the time of day as she was constantly all over Benjamin. They talked to one another like there was no one else in the room, and it made Savannah feel terrible. Penny had been ignoring her ever since they met in Benjamin's home, even at the dinner at their house, she didn't look at her once or say a word to her. It was like she wasn't even there. Savannah hadn't addressed it since she was just so happy to be presented to Benjamin's family. It had to mean that he was serious about her, didn't it? She hoped so. She really liked him a lot, except when he was with his sister. When she was around, it was like he forgot everything about Savannah, and his sister did the same to her date. And it wasn't just the fact that they completely ignored their dates, it was also the way they looked at one another that made Savannah feel uneasy. Both of them had that look that people who were newly in love had. They giggled at each other's jokes and touched each other constantly on the shoulders or the thighs, and sometimes they even held hands.

"She hates me, Benjamin," Savannah said. "Do we have to bring her every time?"

Penny and her new boyfriend had been with them on every date since the day at Benjamin's house. At first, Savannah had thought it was a good idea since it was a way for her to get to know Penny and hopefully get her to like her over time, but as the dates came and went, she had realized that wasn't why Penny was there. It wasn't to hang out with her boyfriend, either. It was to be close to her brother and make sure he and Savannah didn't get a moment alone.

"She doesn't hate you. I promise you," he said and looked her in the eyes. Then he leaned over and kissed her. He tasted heavenly, she thought, and closed her eyes. When she opened them again, Penny stood right in front of her, staring at her, her eyes flaring.

Startled, Savannah pulled back with a light gasp. Seeing this, Penny sat down on her brother's lap with a smile; she threw her arms around his neck and laughed, while her own date didn't even get a glance. Benjamin laughed too, then tickled his sister till she whined with joy, then Penny put her head on his chest with a deep sigh, and said, "I'll never get a man as good as you."

The sentence made Benjamin laugh out loud, while Savannah felt like she was about to choke on her food. She looked down at her pasta dish, then decided she had lost her appetite. She got up and walked outside without a word to anyone. A second later, Benjamin came outside after her.

"What's going on?" he said. "You just left? It was kind of rude?"

"Really? I'm being rude?" she said, fighting to keep her anger at bay. It felt like her throat was swelling up, and no matter how many deep breaths she took, it wouldn't go away.

"Yes, you. Can you please tell me what's going on? I thought we were having a good time."

"What is the deal with your sister and you?" she asked.

Benjamin sighed. His shoulders slumped. "Oh, no, not again. Why do girls always get jealous of my sister?"

"I'm not jealous of her," Savannah said. "I'm freaking out because she treats you like you're her boyfriend, constantly touching you and laughing at your every joke. She never disagrees with you; do you realize that? It doesn't matter what you say, and she even picks the same meals as you. You never ever fight. What siblings don't fight?"

Benjamin stared at her with confused eyes. "You're angry because I don't fight with my sister? I don't understand you. You have to admit; it is a strange thing to be angry about, right?"

Savannah looked into his eyes and felt her knees go soft. What was it about this boy that made her constantly forget that she was angry with him? Could it be that she was falling in love with him?

"You really don't see it, do you?" she asked. "You genuinely have no idea what I'm upset about."

He sighed and grabbed her hands in his. "Listen. I don't always understand you, but I do know that I am falling for you. Big time. I'm doing my best here, so please cut me some slack. Please, don't let this come between us. Please. I'll stop bringing her on our dates. I only did it to help her out a little, and maybe so you two could bond, but she doesn't have to be there all the time if you don't want her to. I will do anything to make this work, Savannah, to make us work. What do you say?"

Savannah looked into his emerald green eyes and felt how all the piled-up anger immediately dissipated. There was no way she could remain angry with him. She was already in too deep for that.

"Please, give me another chance?" he said, smiling like he already knew she would say yes.

She exhaled, leaned forward, and kissed him. "But it's just the two of us from now on, okay? I know you love your sister, but I don't want to share you with her."

He nodded and kissed her again. "You got it."

18

"Austin, please, you have to talk. You have to tell us what happened. You can't just clam up like this."

Shannon looked at Jack from across the living room. They had come back to the cabin, and all the other kids had gone to their rooms while Jack tried to get Austin to open up about what had happened at the ski school. Shannon didn't like how harsh Jack was with Austin. The boy hadn't spoken a word to any of them, not even his twin sister Abigail. He was in shock. Couldn't Jack see that?

"Austin," Jack said and rubbed his forehead. "Come on, boy. Tell me what you saw?"

The boy was looking at his shoes, not his father. They had been at it for at least half an hour, and it was going nowhere. It was getting painful to watch.

"It's me; it's your dad. You can tell me anything," Jack said. "I won't be angry with you if that's what you're afraid of. I just need to hear from you what happened inside that school. It's important for you to talk about this to someone. You can't keep it bottled up. It is also important that the police know the truth. I am gonna ask you one

71

more time; did the instructor shoot himself or did something else happen?"

As Jack said the words, Austin lifted his glare and looked into his father's eyes for the first time. The gesture made Jack gasp lightly.

"He didn't shoot himself, did he? I knew it. Austin, tell me exactly what happened."

But the boy didn't answer. He rose to his feet, then ran off towards the stairs.

"Austin, no!"

Jack ran after him, but Shannon grabbed his arm and stopped him. "Don't, Jack. You're scaring the boy. Can't you see? He's terrified of you."

Jack turned and looked at Shannon. His eyes burned in desperation and anger.

"You stay out of this, Shannon. This doesn't concern you. It's between me and my boy."

Shannon bit her lip, contemplating what to do. She knew Jack was angry right now, but she couldn't just keep quiet. She had to be honest with him, and she had to help Austin. She had bonded with him over hot chocolate today, and that had made her realize that she understood him.

"It does concern me, Jack, and you know it. We're married, remember? We have a family, and we're raising these kids together. I love Austin too, and right now, you're being a detective and not a father. The boy needs your comfort and love; he doesn't need a third-degree interrogation. So what if he chooses not to speak? He's just been through something very traumatic, something that may have scarred him for life. The last thing he needs is to feel like a disappointment to his father. The last thing he needs is for you to be angry with him. That will only make him clam up further."

"So, now you're suddenly the expert on my son, huh?" Jack asked.

Shannon exhaled, calming herself down. "That, I am not. But I do understand him. He's a sensitive boy, a creative soul, and he needs nurturing, not strict discipline and yelling. I know this because that's how I used to be as a child."

Jack glared at her, mouth gaping. Then he shook his head and ran a hand through his hair. "Well, if you think you can do a better job, then be my guest. Go ahead; you talk to him."

"I will," she said, then walked past him up the stairs without another word.

19

How come when it came to my own son I always turned into this monster, this terrible version of myself that reminded me of my old man? I knew it was wrong to pressure him, to yell at him in this situation, yet I still did it. I knew Shannon was right, yet I got angry at her when she told me I was being unreasonable.

I was such a hypocrite.

I stared at my beautiful and wise wife as she disappeared up the stairs, wondering if I should just find a hole and crawl into it. Why was it that all my sense went out the window when I faced my son? It was scary how much I had sounded like my own father just a minute ago. I hated when he yelled at me or when he was disappointed in me. Why was I making my own son feel the same way when I knew how crushing it was to such a young heart? Had I learned nothing from my own experience?

I exhaled and sat in a recliner next to the fireplace, then hid my face between my hands. I felt awful for my son, and the truth was, I was so angry that this had happened to him. This was supposed to be a fun vacation for all of us. I knew it was going to be especially tough on Austin to learn how to snowboard because he often struggled with athletics whereas these things came easily to his sister. All I had wanted was for this to go well for him. I just wanted him to have fun with it, and now this had happened?

What the heck was going on in this town?

First, there was the woman in the car, almost crashing into us. Then there was the boy who had disappeared from next door and his creepy mother in the window, rocking in her chair day and night, waiting for him. And now a nineteen-year-old ski instructor had allegedly shot himself in front of my nine-year-old son?

I grabbed the local paper, *The Mountaineer,* that had been in our mailbox this morning and found the article written about the accident the night before, then found the name of the woman who had driven the car. Eliza Reuben. I wrote it on a piece of paper, then looked at it, wondering who she was.

I then grabbed my laptop and googled her. Tons of links appeared with her name in them, and it didn't take me long to find her Facebook and Instagram profile along with her LinkedIn page.

"She's a journalist," I said to myself and scrolled down her professional profile. "Some pretty big names in here."

"What was that?" Shannon asked as she came down the stairs.

"Nothing," I said. "How did it go with Austin?"

She shrugged and shook her head. "I just hugged him and told him he could come to me anytime when he was ready to talk, but he didn't want to say anything. I told Abigail to stay with him and then put on a movie for them all to watch, to take their minds off things a little. They're all pretty shaken. Tyler doesn't really understand much of what is going on, but he's exhausted from all the skiing and fresh air, so even he sat still and watched the movie. What are you doing? You said something just when I came down?"

"Thank you," I said and looked at her with gratefulness.

"For what? I didn't get him to talk."

I grabbed her hand in mine and put it against my cheek. "Just for being you. I don't know what I would do without you. And you're right. I think you understand Austin better than I do."

Shannon chuckled and sat next to me on the couch with a deep sigh. "So, what are you up to, Jack? And don't try and talk about something else. I know that look in your eyes."

"I just looked up that woman from last night, the one in the car that crashed."

"And? What did you find?" Shannon asked, putting her feet up on the coffee table.

"She's a journalist and not just some random local journalist. She's quite big around here. She's written stuff for *Time Magazine* and all the big ones, and listen to this; she's won a Pulitzer Prize once for her investigative journalism. It was twenty years ago, but still pretty impressive."

Shannon looked surprised. "So, what was she doing out here in the mountains?"

I shrugged. "If you ask the police, she killed someone and then crashed as she tried to escape."

"I have a feeling you don't believe that anymore," she said.

"There are many reasons why she could have the man's blood on her hands and clothes. Just sayin'.'"

"But, certainly, the police must have other things on her to accuse her of killing him?" Shannon said.

I nodded. She had a point. They had to have been investigating her deeper. If only I knew what they had found.

Shannon looked out the window and spotted the woman in the top window of the house next door, sitting in her rocking chair.

"She's still up there, the poor thing. I hate seeing it."

"I know," I said. "Waiting for him to come back. It's heartbreaking. I can't stand looking at her. How long do you think she'll be sitting up there?"

Shannon turned to look at me. "Imagine it was Austin who hadn't been home for three weeks. How long would you sit up there and wait for him to come home?"

I exhaled. "You've got a point. I heard that they searched for him for the first two weeks, combing through the creek and the mountains, but found no trace. I guess after that there is nothing left but to wait."

"What do you think happened to him?" Shannon asked.

I sighed. "Hopefully, he just ran away from home. He's the age for that. But they say a girl broke up with him the night he disappeared. Some people in town fear that he committed suicide, maybe by throwing himself in the creek, and the body just hasn't resurfaced yet. I read in the paper that most people in town blame the girl. Either she killed him, they say, or she broke his heart, and he killed himself. Either way, she's to blame in their eyes."

"Sure can't be fun being her right now," Shannon said with an exhale. "Living in a small town like this with nowhere to escape to."

"Nope. And it won't be less fun should his body show up. The way it is now, there's still the chance that he simply ran away, but should he turn up dead, then people won't forgive the girl."

PART II

20

She didn't go out much anymore and skipped school on days when she simply couldn't face those accusing eyes that seemed constantly to follow her wherever she went.

At the high school, they talked about Savannah from the moment she set her red sneakers in the hallway. Eyes followed her every move, and people turned their back on her if she tried to come near them. The worst time was lunch, where she found herself eating alone day after day while people whispered behind her back, some with small gasps in awe of the girl they believed had killed her own boyfriend.

The school had called the day before and told her mother that Savannah had missed too many classes lately and she needed to come in if she didn't want to risk having to retake the entire year. As she was sitting in class, waiting for the first-period teacher to arrive, something touched the back of her head. Savannah lifted her hand and felt her hair. Her fingers came back with what appeared to be the leftovers of a glazed donut. Savannah turned to look at a group of students behind her.

"Who did this?" she growled.

The kids in the group behind her pulled back in fear. Savannah saw it in their eyes and felt like crying. Did they really think that she was capable of hurting them? Was this what it had come to?

The teacher arrived, and Savannah decided to let it go. She found a napkin and wiped the rest of the donut out of her hair, then found her books and tried to focus. Behind her, she could hear voices whispering.

"I bet she pushed him in the creek."

"I think he's buried in a cave in the mountains."

"Did you see the way she looked at you? That girl is capable of anything. I say she cooked him and ate him."

Savannah sighed and opened her book, then concentrated on what the teacher was saying, but it was hard when she felt like breaking down and crying. This had been going on for three weeks now; was it ever going to end? Would her life ever go back to normal?

WHERE'S BENJAMIN?

The banner was still hanging outside in the courtyard of the school. The wind had torn it at the edges, and it was only stuck to the wall on the top corners now, but the words still rang in her mind. For the most part, when she walked through town, people whispered behind her back, but this very morning as she walked toward school, someone had yelled those exact words at her.

"Where's Benjamin, Savannah?"

Savannah hadn't been able to answer them, just like she hadn't been able to answer that same question when the sheriff had asked her. They had taken her in for questioning twenty-four hours after they realized he was gone. Sheriff Franklin had asked her again and again about Benjamin, and Savannah had answered him repeatedly saying the same thing, feeling crushed that he didn't believe her.

"I haven't seen him since last night when I left him on the porch. I texted him and asked him to come out on the porch with me. I said I needed to talk to him."

"And that's when you broke up with him?"

"Yes. I had waited all night to find the courage to tell him that I didn't want to be with him anymore. It was over and had been for a long while. I don't love him anymore."

"That's a pretty tough statement to swallow for a young boy. It can be crushing to be broken up with. How was his state of mind when you left him?" the sheriff asked.

"His state of mind? I don't know...I guess he was upset and angry."

"So, he got angry when you broke up with him?"

"Yes. He was upset with me. We had a fight. And then I left."

"Were you angry with him?"

"I...I guess."

"Did you kill him? Did you get angry with him and then kill him?"

The question felt like a punch to her stomach. It would be a lie to say that it took her by surprise. She knew what people thought in this town and, of course, they had to ask. But that didn't mean it didn't hurt.

"No," she said shaking her head desperately. "I could never... He was still alive when I left. The last time I saw him was while I was driving out of his driveway. He was still standing on the porch. Wait...you don't think...oh, dear God; do you think he might have... hurt himself because of what I did?"

"We don't know yet," Sheriff Franklin said. "So far, all we know is that he is missing and apparently you were the last person to see him. Who else was in the house that evening?"

"His sister and her boyfriend. And then his parents, of course, but they had already turned in. It was Saturday, and his dad had to get up early as usual on Sundays to preach."

"Did anyone else fight with him that night or did he seem out of sorts in any way?"

Savannah looked at her fingers, then shook her head. "No. It was just me. He was fine till I broke up with him."

.   .   .

Now, as she sat in the classroom, staring at the poster swaying in the freezing wind outside, she couldn't stop wondering if Benjamin's disappearance would end up destroying her life. So far, it had turned it into a living hell for her. She spent most of her time inside the trailer, afraid of leaving it, and she had begun to hate the sight of her prison. She couldn't leave town since the police had told her to stay put, and she couldn't stay either. Every day, she waited for news and feared it at the same time. She had hoped it would pass, that people would eventually stop talking about them, but so far, it had only gotten worse as the days progressed. She couldn't even go to Joey's Pancake House or the Dollar General without people staring at her or saying stuff to her that would make her want to cry. They truly believed she had killed him or at least driven him to suicide. Benjamin was the most popular boy at school and in town. He was the local hero, the sweet preacher's boy, the one everyone loved, whereas Savannah was just a newcomer from out of town, someone no one cared for. If Benjamin's body turned up, she was definitely going to be lynched.

21

None of us slept much that night. I was staring at the ceiling while Shannon was tossing and turning next to me. I kept wondering about that kid at the ski school. He had been no more than nineteen years old. He had his whole life in front of him. No matter how I turned it, I simply couldn't fathom that this could be a suicide. The look in Austin's eyes when I asked him about it told me I was right, and I couldn't let it go.

As daybreak came, I took a shower, then hurried downstairs to get the newspaper from the mailbox. I glanced briefly at Mrs. Rutherford in the tower window, then rushed inside before my cheeks froze to ice. Tyler had come down with a handful of cars in his arms and sat in front of the fireplace, playing. Shannon came down soon after while I was in the middle of the article about Lyle Bishop, the graduate of Maggie Valley High, who was working as a ski instructor at the Cataloochee Ski Area and who was supposed to start college after the summer. He lived outside of town on his parent's farm, and the newspaper had interviewed a neighbor who said the family was in deep shock. Lyle had never shown any sign of depression; he was a happy boy and known to take very good care of the children at the ski school.

He was by far the best one to handle the younger children, one of his colleagues was quoted saying. *He was like a big child himself, always goofing around and making the children laugh.*

"So, why should we believe he killed himself?" I mumbled as Shannon pulled out a pan for making pancakes. "And in front of a child he knew would be scarred for life. It makes no sense."

Shannon placed a hand on my shoulder. "Why don't you make some sense out of it?"

"What do you mean?" I asked, even though I already knew. "What about our vacation? What about the children?"

She sighed and tilted her head. "You're not going to get any rest anyway, and neither are we. The kids don't want to go back there today, and I can't blame them. They need a break. I do too. We're just going to hang out here today anyway. You go do what you need to do."

I swallowed, feeling all kinds of love for my wife. I couldn't believe how well she knew me. I leaned over and kissed her cheek.

"Thank you, sweetie."

"A peck on the cheek isn't going to be enough, you know," she said and grabbed my chin and pulled me into a real kiss. As our lips parted and she looked me in the eyes, she said, "Now, that's better."

I heard chatter and footsteps on the steps above us, then smiled and grabbed my phone.

"I have a phone call to make, but I'll take it on the porch, so you and the kids can be as noisy as you want. Be back in a sec."

"Don't forget your jacket; it's freezing out there," Shannon said.

I grabbed the jacket off the hanger, then put it on with a smile. Phone clutched against my ear, I closed the door and stepped out into the crisp air and tapped a number. A familiar voice came on the phone.

"Rebekka Franck."

"Hi, Rebekka," I said with an exhale. "It's Jack. I need your help with something."

22

Shannon let me take the car to the hospital since she and the kids were just staying in today. Haywood Regional Medical Center was located about eight miles from downtown Maggie Valley, so I figured I could do it fast and be back in time for lunch. Abigail made me promise I'd bring back some ice cream. I didn't quite understand how anyone could eat ice cream in this cold, but Abigail had insisted and told me that there was so much I didn't understand anyway.

How could I argue with that?

They had put up a guard at Eliza Reuben's room and, as I approached him with my badge in my hand, I realized it was Deputy Winston.

"Ryder, my man," he said and shook my hand. "How's the kid?"

"To be honest, he's not doing very well. He hasn't spoken a word to any of us, not even his twin sister. He didn't come down this morning for breakfast, and it worried me."

"That's a bummer, man. I am so sorry. I am sure he'll get better, though. He's probably just in a state of deep shock."

I nodded. "I know. It's just tough when it's your own kid, you know?"

Winston shook his head. "I still can't believe Lyle would do that in front of him."

"You knew Lyle well?" I asked.

"You could say that. He used to be friends with my little brother, Anthony. They practically grew up together. He never seemed like someone who would end himself like that, but I guess that's what they always say, right?"

"I guess."

Deputy Winston looked down at the bouquet of daisies in my hand. I had bought them at a small flower shop on my way there.

"Are you here to see her?" Winston asked and nodded toward the door.

"I thought I'd check in on her. Any news?"

Winston shook his head. "Still the same. Take a look for yourself."

He pushed the door open, so I could walk inside. Eliza was lying pale in her bed, monitors beeping next to her and tubes in her nose and throat. I had seen her picture under the byline of the articles I had read and on her social media profiles, but this didn't look much like that woman. Once again, I was reminded how lucky we had all been that she didn't hit us, and once again, I thought about that black pick-up truck I had seen on the scene.

Winston left me, then came back with a vase for my flowers, and I put them in water.

"Does she have any family?" I asked.

Winston nodded. "A mother who can't leave the house and a brother who's a drunk and that we haven't been able to locate. We went to her apartment and found an old dog that we took to a shelter."

"Did you find anything else there?" I asked, fishing for details of the case. "Do you have a motive yet?"

Winston shook his head. "We don't, no. We don't know what she was doing at Harry's place."

"Harry, huh? And how did Harry die?"

"He was shot in the chest, and her fingerprints were all over the weapon. We found it in the living room, a few feet away from the body."

"Really?" I asked.

Winston nodded. "Yeah. Now, all we need is for her to wake up so we can get her to confess and then this will hopefully be all over."

23

Back in the car, I found my phone and started to search for Harry's and other recent deaths in Maggie Valley. Soon, I found a couple of small notes in the local media of the finding of a Harry Mayer in his home, the same night that Eliza Reuben crashed her car. Nowhere did I find that the police linked the two stories to one another, so it hadn't been made public yet.

"Harry Mayer," I said out loud in the car. "Who were you and why did you have to die?"

It had started to snow again, and I watched the flakes dancing in the air before hitting my windshield, then my phone rang. I saw Rebekka's name on the display, then picked up. Rebekka Franck was a journalist from Cocoa Beach who had recently helped me solve the case of ten missing girls from our local school. She had also recently been involved in another murder case in Webster in Central Florida and gotten herself hurt so badly that she ended up in a wheelchair, but only for a few weeks, the doctors had promised her.

"Hi there. You got news for me?"

"I sure do," she said.

"I know you're supposed to be in recovery, but I was desperate for help and figured you could give me what I needed."

"Are you kidding me? It's not like I have anything better to do. You have no idea how helpless I feel in this thing. I get so bored in the house when the kids are in school all day, and with nothing to do. Making a few phone calls can hardly tire me out. Besides, it felt good to use my brain a little, so don't you feel sorry. I'm happy to help."

I smiled and held the phone close to my ear. I had been so scared when I heard what had happened to her back there and had to admit that, even though she could be quite annoying, I had grown to care about her.

"So, what have you got?" I asked. "You said you found something?"

"I made a few calls around to some of my colleagues and, apparently, Eliza was working on quite a big story in Maggie Valley, North Carolina. She lives in one of the neighboring towns and threw herself at the story as soon as it turned up. The story went national for a few days before something else turned up, but my colleague at *Time*, the magazine she was working on the story for, said it was something pretty big. She had recently had a big breakthrough and had told their editor to make room for it in next month's issue. That was before the accident, of course. The story was about the disappearance of a young boy named Benjamin Rutherford. Does that ring a bell?"

I leaned back in my seat. "It most certainly does. Did they know exactly what she was working on?"

"I'm sorry. They can't reveal that, especially not to another journalist. They probably won't tell a detective either. If it's as good as I got the feeling it was, then they're not revealing anything. Eliza probably didn't even tell anyone either. She can't risk anyone blabbing to another journalist from some other magazine or stealing the story for themselves."

"Wonderful business you're in," I said.

"I know. It's nasty. Can't turn your back on anyone without returning with a knife in it. I still love it, though. Don't ask me why.

Anyway, I should get going. I have a hair appointment in an hour, and Sune has promised to take me there."

"Are you guys back together?" I asked, concerned. The last I heard, her boyfriend Sune had cheated on her, and they had broken up.

"No. He's just helping me now that I can't get around on my own. Anyway, let me know if I can do anything else for you, okay?"

"Thanks."

I hung up, then looked at the display, thinking about Eliza and her story. It was something big, she had said. Had she made a discovery of some sort in the case that no one else knew about?

I started up the engine, remembering the laptop I had seen in the front seat of her car when I pulled her out. It had probably contained all her work, her research, and interviews. But it had been completely destroyed in the crash. It didn't look like it could be recovered.

24

"Austin? Are you in there?"

Shannon knocked gently on the door to the children's room, but no answer came. She hadn't seen Austin all morning, and he hadn't come down for breakfast. She had spoken to Abigail, who said that her brother had decided to stay in the room. He hadn't told her why and he still hadn't said a word to her about the incident. Shannon had decided to give him some space, then fed the other children and cleaned up after them before she decided she had to go check on him and make sure he was all right.

"Austin?" she said again and knocked a second time, but still there was no answer, so she opened the door carefully and peeked inside. She spotted Austin sitting on the bed, looking out the window.

"Austin? Are you okay?"

He didn't turn his head to look at her, so she walked in, careful to not step on all the bags and clothes on the floor. She picked up one of Angela's shirts and folded it, then placed it on top of her suitcase. Then she sat down next to him on the bed. She looked out the window, trying to figure out if he was actually looking at something or if he was just lost in his thoughts. In the neighboring yard, she spotted a man gathering firewood and guessed that had to be Mr. Rutherford, the local pastor whose son had gone missing. She lifted her glance to look at his wife, who was still sitting in the window of the small tower, rocking back and forth. Shannon wondered if she ever slept. She had to get some sleep and food at some point, right?

Poor thing.

"Aren't you hungry at all?" Shannon asked. "I made pancakes with chocolate chips in them, your favorite."

Austin shook his head, then looked down at his socks.

"I can bring them to you if you prefer to eat up here."

He shook his head again. It broke Shannon's heart to see him like this. He had always been the quiet one of the twins, but still. This was too much. It was torture to witness. Part of her wanted to tell him to drop it, to just start speaking, but the other part, the one that remembered what it was like to be a child like that, knew it was best to take it calmly and not get upset with him. He needed her to be understanding and caring. No one had understood that about Shannon when she was a child and shut up like a clam whenever things got tough. It had happened after her dad left. Shannon had loved her father more than anyone on this Earth and never felt very close with her mother, so it broke her heart more than any of her sisters' that he would just leave and never look back. Shannon had stopped speaking for almost a year and drove everyone around her nuts with her silence, especially her mother. When she finally started to make sounds with her mouth again, it had come out as singing, and after that, she had never really stopped. She preferred singing over talking any day and often felt like she could express herself better through music than through any other means of communication. Later in her life, the not speaking had been her way of reacting when things got bad, like when her mother beat her up or after her uncle had molested her, or after her brother accidentally shot himself. She would pull into her own world and simply not speak to anyone. But the singing, she couldn't stop anymore. Music had to get out of her, no matter how hurt she was, and soon she found out that singing was a way better weapon than silence because it meant she didn't keep it all bottled up inside anymore. She got it all out.

Now, she wondered if Austin might feel the same way. She looked at him and started tapping rhythmically on her leg, then began to sing one of her songs that she believed he knew the lyrics to. But as much as she sang her heart out, he didn't join in. He didn't even look at her but kept staring out the window like she wasn't even there, and slowly the song died out. Shannon stopped it with an exhale.

"Guess you're not in the mood for singing, huh? Or eating or talking. Is there anything I can do?" She paused and waited. "I guess not."

Shannon was almost by the door, ready to leave when the boy suddenly made a sound. To her disappointment he wasn't talking, nor was he singing. What came out of him was ear-piercingly loud and made the hairs stand up on her neck.

25

Maggie Valley 2017

They went back to his house after dinner. His parents weren't home, he said. They turned on the TV and watched a movie, snuggling up on the couch. Savannah felt a sigh of relief rush through her body as they kissed. Benjamin had kept his promise to her and the past couple of weeks had been wonderful between them. She finally felt like he was all hers.

"Do you want something to drink?" he asked as their lips parted and they looked into each other's eyes. She felt such warmth and knew in this instant that there was no way back anymore. She was falling for him. Now the falling, in itself, wasn't the problem; it was when you hit the ground that the trouble began. That's when you got hurt, and Savannah had been hurt badly before. She pulled away with a light gasp, suddenly afraid of what was happening to her, fearful of repeating her old mistakes.

"Are you okay?" he asked. "You just looked like you wanted to run away or something."

The movie continued on the TV, but they weren't watching it anymore. Savannah looked into Benjamin's eyes. Did she dare to give her heart to him? Did she dare to go all in and risk getting hurt again?

Her shoulders came down as she once again looked into his soft eyes and saw his gentle smile. No, Benjamin wasn't like that. He would never hurt her.

"I'm okay," she said. "Just a little tired; that's all."

"Let me get you a soda," he said.

He was about to get to his feet when Savannah stopped him. Determined not to let her past pain destroy what she had right now, she pulled him close, then kissed him deeply and intensely, wanting to let him know how deeply she was falling for him, how much she wanted him.

Benjamin grinned as their lips parted. "Wowzah."

Savannah smiled and let go of him. "Now, go get that soda, will you?"

"You betcha," he said and winked, then jumped off the couch and disappeared toward the kitchen.

Savannah sat up and wiped her lips, then chuckled happily as the main character in the movie finally got the woman he had been longing for and they kissed. Savannah thought about Benjamin and couldn't stop smiling, not until she saw something reflected in the TV, or rather someone. Savannah gasped lightly, then turned her head and spotted Penny behind her. She was standing in the doorway, a soda can in her hand, glaring at Savannah.

How long has she been standing there? Has she been watching us while we were making out?

Benjamin came back with a Coke in his hand, then stopped as he saw her too. "Oh, hey, Penny. I didn't see you there."

Penny stared at both of them, eyes scorching, then turned around and stormed off.

Savannah looked at Benjamin, debating if she should say anything or simply stay out of it. It seemed to be a thing between him and his sister.

"Someone's in a bad mood," he said with a shrug, then handed

Savannah the can with a shrug. He sat down next to her, and they continued watching the movie. A few minutes in, his phone buzzed, and he picked it up. He held it so Savannah couldn't see the display, then read the text before putting it down on the couch again.

They watched the movie, but Savannah couldn't stop thinking about Penny or about the text he had received, and later, as he ran for the bathroom, she picked up his phone and saw that he had received another text. It was from Penny, and the text said:

ARE YOU COMING TO BED SOON?

What the...?

Benjamin returned from the bathroom, smiling at her, then leaned over to kiss her. Savannah stopped him and pulled away.

"What's wrong?" he asked. "Did I do something?"

"Why is your sister asking you if you're coming to bed soon?" she asked. "I saw the text on your phone."

Benjamin sat back down with a shrug. "She sleeps in my bed sometimes. She thinks her own room is too scary; that's all. She suffers from terrible nightmares sometimes."

"And your parents are okay with that?" Savannah asked, puzzled. She had never had any siblings, so she didn't know whether this was normal at their age. It made her stomach uneasy, but she didn't know if it was just her.

"Sure. It's always been like that."

26

Shannon stormed outside, not even caring enough to put on her coat. The cold didn't matter; she barely felt it with all the adrenaline and fear rushing through her veins.

She ran across the snow, toward the creek, running through the backyard of the property they had rented. She stopped as she reached the dock that was shared between their cabin and the house next door, then knelt on the wood, heart pounding against her ribs.

Oh, dear God, no. Oh, dear God!

What Shannon had seen from the window had been nothing but an odd dark shape floating midstream. Austin had seen it first, then began to scream. Shannon had felt like screaming too but instead told the boy to stay put, while she ran to see what it was. In her heart, she had known right away, just like Austin knew when he saw it. But in her mind, she had prayed that it wasn't it, that it was something else. As she came closer, the shape had turned into a body...the body of a young man floating on his stomach. His blond hair was spread out in the water, shaping what looked like a halo around his head. Shannon found it hard to breathe. The creek was carrying the body away, and

Shannon feared it would soon get lost. She bent forward and reached out her arm to try and grab it as it floated by. She managed to get her fingers on his belt and pull him toward the dock. She then grabbed him by the shoulders and pulled him up, grunting and panting with effort. His body was heavy and hard to maneuver, but finally, she succeeded. The heavy body plunked down on the wooden dock. Shannon fumbled with the weight of the body, then turned it around to look at the face. She stared at the pale face, then exhaled deeply, recognizing him from the photo in the paper.

Thinking she'd better call Jack, she rose to her feet when she spotted someone, a figure standing at the end of the dock. It was a woman. Her face was pale from weeks of barely any sleep and no sunlight, her hair and clothes raggedy and scruffy, but you could still see that she used to be someone who took care of herself.

Mrs. Rutherford stood like a statue and stared at the body on the dock. Her eyes were stained with tears, but more frozen in shock than moved by what she saw.

"Is it him?"

She spoke in an even tone with no sense of urgency like had she asked Shannon what time it was or how to find her way downtown.

Shannon swallowed, searching for the words. How did you tell a mother you had found her dead son?

"Yes."

Mrs. Rutherford nodded. She remained frozen in place, her hands shaking slightly while more people came running down from the house. Her husband put a coat on Mrs. Rutherford's shoulders, while a girl stopped next to her, an air of complete shock on her face. The girl clasped her mouth with a light gasping sound while her shoulders dropped. She was fighting to breathe. Pastor Rutherford told them all to stay back, then approached Shannon, his steps slowing down as he came closer to the body. He knelt next to it, then removed a lock of wet hair from Benjamin's face.

It was like the air went out of him and he dropped down, his hand touching the face gently. Behind him, Mrs. Rutherford had to be held up by her daughter.

"My boy," the pastor said. "My beautiful, beautiful boy."

27

I drove up the driveway; then I spotted the crowd that had gathered by the dock. I saw Shannon standing among them, talking to the pastor. It wasn't until I killed the engine that I spotted the body.

I opened the door and rushed toward them. As Shannon saw me, I could see the immediate relief on her face.

"Jack, my husband, is a detective," she said and urged me to come closer. I couldn't get my eyes off the dead body. I approached it and knelt next to it, studying it closely. I tried to keep my poor beating heart calm as I recognized his face from the pictures I had seen.

"We found him in the creek," Shannon said. I could tell she was fighting to keep it together. "He was floating by...right out there."

"I am so sorry for your loss," I said addressed to the Pastor and Mrs. Rutherford. Their youngest, who had to be Penelope, was clinging to her mother's shoulder, crying, while the oldest, Charles Jr. had wheeled his chair onto the porch behind us where he stayed, unable to get into the yard because of the thick snow. He looked to be in his mid-twenties.

"I'll call the sheriff and have them come out here."

I put the phone to my ear, then walked away, despair welling in my throat. No matter how often I had seen it, I could never get used to looking into the eyes of a parent who had just lost their child. I couldn't help myself; I kept thinking about my own children and how I would feel if it had been one of them. I took a deep breath to calm myself down and focus on my conversation when Sheriff Franklin came to the phone.

"Detective Ryder? What's up?"

"We found him," I said, almost losing the fight with my tears. "We found your boy in the creek."

A silence occurred before he said, "We'll be right there."

I hung up, pressing back the tears burning my eyes, then locked eyes with Shannon. She approached me.

"They're on their way," I said in a low voice. "Shouldn't be long. How are you coping? How are the kids?"

"Kids are fine. Austin was the one who saw it, though. He started to scream, and that's how I saw it too. Then I ran out here. I told them all to stay inside. I can see them all in the window, though. They're watching us."

I sighed tiredly. "They're just curious. But they shouldn't be dealing with any of this. This is our vacation, for crying out loud. They're supposed to be worrying about falling on their skis or snowboard or what to eat for lunch. Not dead bodies floating by outside their windows."

"I'm sure they'll be okay. We'll talk to them when we get back."

I touched Shannon's cheek. "You didn't answer my other question. How are you holding up?"

She lifted both eyebrows for a brief second. "I'm shocked, to be honest. But I guess that I'll be all right. I'm the lucky one, remember? I still have all my children. I am not the one who has lost her child."

Shannon glanced at Mrs. Rutherford as she spoke the last word. In the distance, we could hear sirens approaching, and seconds later, the driveway was packed with police cruisers. I watched the sheriff get out of his and approach us, walking with heavy steps in his boots.

He shook my hand.

"They found him drifting down the creek," I said and walked with him toward Benjamin Rutherford's body. "My wife spotted him from the window and ran down here. The family must have seen it too because they came down soon after."

Sheriff Franklin exhaled and took off his hat, then approached Benjamin. He knelt next to him for a few seconds, then nodded and went over to the Rutherfords, still holding his hat between his hands.

"I am so sorry for your loss. This was not the ending I wanted. You have my deepest sympathies."

Mrs. Rutherford wept in her daughter's embrace, while Pastor Rutherford stared at the sheriff, shifting on his feet, his nostrils flaring lightly, his eyes on fire.

"She did it," he said.

"Charles!" his wife exclaimed. "Our son's body is barely cold, and already you're throwing mud at his girlfriend. I will not have you stoop so low; do you hear me? That is not how we do things in our family."

Pastor Rutherford turned to face his wife, shaking his head. "Don't call her that. She is not his girlfriend; she's a murderer. She killed him, and you know it as well as I do. She smelled like trouble from the moment I saw her. I knew she would end up destroying him."

"That doesn't mean she hurt him. Besides, your son was no saint, and you know it."

"Why are you protecting her?" Pastor Rutherford asked. "You never liked her either. You always said she was wrong for our boy, so why are you so busy defending her?"

"I'm not defending anyone. I'm merely saying that there is no reason for us to go around blaming anyone either. And just because I didn't like her, that doesn't mean it's okay to blame her for something she had no hand in. We can't blame her for our son's suicide."

Pastor Rutherford pointed his finger at his wife. "He did not kill himself. I will not have you say such a thing. No son of mine would kill himself. Especially not him, not my Benjamin."

His father's words sparked a reaction from the older brother, who turned around and rolled back inside the house.

"Just stop it, both of you, will you?" Penny yelled. "Benjamin is dead. He's gone. The police are here. They'll find out whether he killed himself or he was murdered."

"He was murdered," Pastor Rutherford said, speaking through tears. His torso was now trembling in spasms. "And she did this. Mark my words. She did this to him."

I glanced at Shannon and signaled her. She understood my intention.

"Let me take you all back to the house," she said. "The police are going to take over now. Let's let them do their job."

28

Shannon helped Mrs. Rutherford sit down in a chair by the window inside their living room. She said she wanted to sit where she could keep an eye on what went on outside. Her daughter sat next to her, holding her hand. Pastor Rutherford kept pacing back and forth, grumbling to himself, sounding almost like he was arguing with someone.

"Will you stop that, Charles?" Beatrice Rutherford said. "You're making us all nervous."

He walked to the window and peeked out. A crowd had gathered as some of the locals were arriving to see, and the police had set up a perimeter to make sure no one came too close and ruined evidence. Shannon could see Jack as he knelt next to the body with Sheriff Franklin. They were pointing and talking vividly. An ambulance had arrived, and a guy Shannon guessed was the coroner was now rushing across the snow, a bag in his hand. Shannon didn't know much about crime scene investigation, but Jack had told her a few details.

"Why are they not arresting her?" Pastor Rutherford said. "Why are they still here?"

"Will you let it go, Charles?" his wife said. "This is a time for grief, nothing else. Our son is dead; do you hear me? He's dead; he's gone. He'll never come back through that door and smile at us all again. He'll never hug me; he'll never...never tell me..." Beatrice Rutherford stopped herself and sank back into the chair, head bent.

Penny Rutherford pulled her into a deep hug, and the mother wept in her embrace. Meanwhile, the pastor couldn't find peace. He tried to sit down for a few seconds, but then got back up again and continued pacing.

"He broke up with her right before it happened," Pastor Rutherford said between tears. "Penny heard them fighting. "

Shannon wondered what to do with herself. She was worried about the children and wanted to get back to them, but at the same time, she wasn't sure these people would be all right or whether it was appropriate to leave them like this. They seemed to be falling apart. Even Penny, who hugged her mother, was sobbing loudly and her was body trembling. Shannon felt out of place and helpless, and she got herself ready to leave. The kids needed her, and at some point, the police would want to talk to her about how she found the body for their report. Jack had told her so.

"I have to...I should be getting back to my children. Again, I am so very sorry for your loss."

They didn't even notice her. The pastor was the only one who gave her a look and nodded. Shannon then hurried to the door and went outside on the porch. She breathed a few times, trying to get rid of the tight sensation in her chest. As she took a second to herself, someone else appeared on the porch. The sound of the wheels rolling across the wood made her turn and look.

It was Charles Junior.

"You scared me," she said.

"I'm sorry," he said. "I didn't mean to. I just needed a little air. You know it was right here, where you're standing, that I saw him last?"

She tilted her head. "On the porch?"

Charles Junior nodded with a sniffle. It was hard to tell because he was sitting down, but he seemed to be a short guy like his brother and father. He had dark hair like his father, not blond like the rest of the family.

"You were with him on the night he disappeared?" Shannon asked.

"I wasn't with him. I was watching him...and her. From over there. I like to come out here sometimes and just watch the stars, and they didn't know I was there. They were busy arguing."

"And what were they arguing about?" Shannon asked.

Charles Junior shook his head. "Usual stuff. She said she didn't want to date him anymore."

"*She* didn't want to date him anymore?" Shannon asked, puzzled since the father had just said it was the other way around. Shannon decided the brother had to know better since he had actually been out there with them.

Charles nodded. "She seemed so angry at him and kept yelling. Anyway, I didn't feel comfortable being there and listening in on their conversation, so I rolled out into the light toward the door. Savannah saw me and started to yell at me for eavesdropping. She pushed my shoulder and told me I was a helpless idiot; I always had been, ever since..."

"That sounds awful. So, what did you say?" Shannon asked, baffled.

"I knew she never liked me much, so I tried to ignore her. She never liked anyone in our family. I just told her to take care of her own problems and went inside. Once I was inside, they continued their argument, and I went to bed. But now I get so angry at myself for not having told Benjamin to get back inside. She was so aggressive. I should have protected him. I just never thought she could...I mean you don't think she'd hurt him, right? They were just arguing. The thing is, she was right. I was weak. I didn't do anything while I had the chance. Why couldn't I act more like a big brother? I should have told him it was too cold out there or told him it was too late, something. Instead, I just left them there, and now he's...gone. I hate this stupid chair."

Shannon bit her lip and nodded. She wondered why he was telling her all this. Was it because his heart was heavy with guilt? Was there more to what he was saying? It seemed like he was holding something back—like he was carrying some weight heavier than what he was letting out.

"Do you know what he and his girlfriend were fighting about?" Shannon asked.

Charles shook his head. "Probably just the usual stuff. They fought often. Savannah found it hard to deal with the fact that Benjamin was very close to his sister. It was an issue she often brought up, and I guess she finally had enough and broke it off with him."

"So, you're telling me she broke up with him because he was too close with his sister?"

Charles nodded. "She wasn't the first one with these types of issues. Benjamin's other girlfriends often had the same problem." He glanced toward the creek and the many people gathered by the dock.

"Anyway, I think you might want to get back now," he said and nodded toward their cabin, where Shannon at this moment spotted Abigail rushing out, barefoot in the snow, sprinting toward the crowd, probably eyeing a chance to satisfy her curiosity.

Shannon wanted to thank Charles Junior before she left, but as she turned to look, he was gone. Puzzled at this, she walked into the snow and rushed toward Abigail, calling her name. The girl stopped as she heard her and turned to look.

"Where do you think you're going, young lady?" Shannon asked. "I thought I told you all to stay put inside the house. The police don't need all you kids running around out here destroying important evidence."

Abigail smiled like Shannon had caught her stealing cookies. "Ah, there you are, Shannon. I was just...I was just going to find you. We're all starving; could you come back and make us something to eat?"

29

I stayed with the sheriff for a few hours, helping him and his deputies out in any way I could before I finally went back to the cabin where Shannon and the kids waited for me. Shannon greeted me with a big kiss and Tyler clung to my leg, while the girls seemed too busy even to notice I was home. Betsy Sue was doing Abigail's and Angela's hair and dressing them up. It was a game they played a lot since she came to live with us and one of the few she would participate in.

"You're freezing, Jack," Shannon said and felt my cheeks. "Come. Let me make you some hot chocolate. The rest of us had some earlier."

"You're a lifesaver, thank you," I said and took the cup between my fingers. As soon as I had emptied it, I put wood in the fireplace and lit it. I sat on a couch in front of it, Shannon sitting down next to me.

"So, what happened out there?" she asked. "Did he drown?"

"They don't know for sure yet, but the initial examination doesn't point in that direction. Just by looking at his body, I could see that he hadn't been in the water for the entire three weeks."

Shannon sipped her cup. A little whipped cream remained on her upper lip, and I couldn't help smiling when seeing it. I kissed it away.

"How could you tell that?" she said afterward. "How could you tell that he hadn't been in the water that long?"

"He was in too perfect a condition," I said. "There was no decomposition at all. Three weeks is a long time."

She shrugged. "It's cold out. The water must be freezing; couldn't that have served to preserve him?"

"It could, but there are other factors...like animals. His skin was too smooth. If he had been in the water for this long, there'd have been animals feeding on him, but there was no scavenging at all. Plus, they searched the creek for two entire weeks after his disappearance. They had divers in and everything. They would have found him then."

"So, what are you saying? That someone put him in the water for us to find now? Three weeks later?"

I sighed and looked into the crackling fire. Abigail whined because Betsy Sue was braiding her hair too tightly. Betsy Sue told her it would be a lot easier if she would only sit still like Angela.

"That's what I'm afraid of."

"But who? And does that mean that...he was killed?"

I nodded and looked into her eyes. "There was another thing. He had a bruise on the back of his head. A pretty big one."

Shannon opened her eyes wide. "A bruise? But...but...couldn't he have hurt his head when falling in the creek? On a rock perhaps?"

"It's a possibility, yes. He could have slipped and hurt his head, then drowned, or he could have jumped in intending to kill himself, then hurt his head on a rock underwater. But that doesn't explain why he wasn't found till now. The creek isn't very deep. There's a constant flow to it; his body would have been washed out sooner even if it did go to the bottom first. Plus, fish and other animals would have fed on him, and they hadn't. It just doesn't make any sense if you ask me."

"So, what happens next?"

"They'll investigate and hopefully find the truth. But it might take a while. How's he doing?" I said and looked toward the stairs. "How's Austin?"

Shannon shook her head. "Not too well. He's just sitting up there. He doesn't even talk to Abigail."

"He hasn't been down all day? Has he had anything to eat at all?" I asked.

She shook her head. "I've asked him, but he just shakes his head."

I got up. "I'll make him a sandwich and take it to him."

30

Austin was playing on his phone when I entered carrying a peanut butter and jelly sandwich. He didn't look up, so I went to him and sat down. I held up the plate with the sandwich. Austin gave it a quick glance, then continued playing.

"Ah, come on," I said. "You've got to be a little hungry, right? You haven't eaten all day."

He continued playing, completely ignoring me.

"Austin," I said. "I need you to put that thing down and eat. Now."

Austin continued playing, and I grabbed his phone then pulled it out of his hand. He made an annoyed sound, and I pushed the sandwich at him.

"Eat first, then play later."

Austin sighed, then grabbed the sandwich and took a bite. I watched him chew, wondering what was going on inside that little mind of his. What he had seen the day before was terrible, no doubt about it; I just wondered if there was more to it than what we knew. Was he harboring something inside of him that he needed to tell us?

"So...I was thinking that maybe we should talk a little? About what happened yesterday?" I said, trying to sound easygoing and not pushy. It was hard since I really wanted to push him to tell me what he saw, what really happened. I couldn't fathom why the boy wouldn't just tell me.

"It must have been scary, right? Were you scared?" I asked.

Austin stopped chewing for a second. His eyes met mine, and I could tell he was still frightened.

"It's okay," I said. "It was a scary situation. It's perfectly normal for you to be afraid. Can you tell me if Lyle said anything to you or if something else happened before...?"

Austin continued chewing. His big blue eyes stared at me. I could tell that something was going on inside of him; a myriad of thoughts was rushing through his little mind. He was debating whether or not to talk to me.

"Come on, son. It's okay. You can tell me. Tell me what happened, please."

Austin swallowed the bite, then shook his head, his eyes avoiding mine.

"Please, Austin."

"I can't," he said, speaking so low I could hardly hear it.

I wrinkled my forehead. "You can't? Why not? I don't understand, Austin. Why can't you tell me? Austin?"

I grabbed his arm and then regretted it immediately. The gesture made the boy shut up completely and turn his head away from me once again.

"Austin, please, just talk to me. I promise it doesn't matter what you say; I won't be mad."

I looked at him, waiting for a response; anything would do right now. I wondered if he blamed himself for what happened...if he maybe thought it was his fault that Lyle shot himself.

If he shot himself. You don't really believe he did, do you?

Knowing I had lost the boy once again and pushed too hard, I grabbed the empty plate and rose to my feet. I was about to walk out of the room to give my son some space when I stopped myself. I didn't want to leave the boy to himself up here all alone. It wasn't good for him.

"Say, how about you and I go for a drive, huh? I have to run an errand first, but thought maybe we could look for a donut place? They ought to have one out here somewhere right?"

Austin lifted his eyes, and his face lit up. It warmed me. Austin got down from the bed and rushed to the door, then hurried out.

I shrugged and followed him.

"I'll take that as a yes?"

31

I drove up the narrow street to the neighborhood of Riddle Cove and parked in front of the small picket fence. It wasn't hard to find out where Harry Mayer lived. The house was a small wooden three-story yellow building with a big porch on the back side, facing the creek. In the front yard, there was a snow-covered tree with an empty birdhouse, a small well, and a flagpole holding a huge flag that had been ripped at the edges by the freezing wind.

I left Austin in the car and told him it would only take a few minutes, then walked up the small trail toward the entrance. The front door was up a long set of stairs, and I climbed them, then knocked. I knew no one would probably answer, but thought I'd be polite anyway. Police tape was still dangling on the door, and I crawled underneath it as I opened it.

Inside, I was met with the familiar stench of death. It was thick and acrid, and I held my nose. Large swaths of the carpet inside the living room had been removed by the forensics team, and the exposed floorboards were stained brown from the dried-up blood. From the look of it, there had been a lot of blood.

I knelt next to where the body had been, then looked at where the forensic techs had gathered their evidence. I found the place where the gun had been lying by the wall like Winston had told me. Then I looked at where the body was placed and wondered why on earth Eliza would have left the gun right there with her fingerprints all over it. She was an intelligent woman, and if she was trying to get away with murder, wouldn't she have gotten rid of the murder weapon? Wouldn't she at least have tried to throw it in the creek where the fingerprints might be washed off?

I tried to imagine the scene, where she came in and shot him in the chest while he was still sitting in his chair. There was a lot of blood on the chair, so I assumed that's where he was sitting when he was shot. What puzzled me was the fact that the body was found on the carpet. Had he slid down from the chair?

"Or maybe she pulled him down," I mumbled and walked to the spot where they had removed big chunks of the carpet.

The body was on that carpet for quite some time, judging from how much blood had soaked into it and even reached the floor beneath.

"Why would her hands be covered in blood if she shot him?" I asked myself. "Wouldn't she just have shot him, then left him to die? Why throw the gun away; why touch him? Why pull him onto the carpet and touch him, getting his blood all over her hands?"

I sighed and thought about the night I had pulled Eliza out of the car. My hands had also been covered in blood, her blood. Because I had been performing CPR. I had pressed my hands down on her bloody chest.

Could she have...could Eliza have tried to do the same?

I tried to picture another scenario. I saw her come in and see Harry sitting there, already shot. Desperate to do something, she pulled him down and started to perform CPR, pressing on his chest to get him back to life.

But what about the gun? The gun was found over there by the wall.

"If it was in his hand," I mumbled. "To make it look like suicide.

Just like Lyle had the gun in his hand. Then Eliza would have removed it and thrown it across the floor before pulling the dead man down to the carpet and beginning her attempt to resuscitate him. That's how she got the blood on her fingers and how her fingerprints ended up on the gun. Some of the residue could have rubbed off on her hands as well."

I nodded, thinking it made a lot of sense, a lot more than her killing him, in my opinion. But then another thought hit me.

Why did she run away? Why didn't she at least call for help?

"The black truck," I said, a sense of urgency swelling in my chest. "Someone was after her."

It all made sense now. Eliza came to the house—for whatever reason that I didn't know yet—and found Harry Mayer shot, then tried to revive him when she realized she wasn't alone in the house. The person who killed Harry Mayer was still there when she got here, and whoever it was chased Eliza till she crashed. He had probably thought she was already dead when seeing the smashed up car and driven away. But she didn't die, and he'd have to know that by now. It had been in the papers and even mentioned in the local news broadcast. That meant the killer was still out there, but that also meant that Eliza's life was still in danger.

32

"Hello?"

I looked up as someone came to the door. He pushed it wide open but stayed outside the police tape. His eyes landed on me.

"Excuse me, sir? You can't be here. It's a crime scene."

I rose to my feet and walked to him. He was an older man, dressed in a thick winter coat and a beanie. I approached him with a friendly smile, reaching inside my pocket for my badge.

"It's okay," I said and showed it to him. "I'm a detective."

The man seemed to relax. His eyes grew friendly. "Oh, okay. I'm sorry then. I just saw you go in from my window and wanted to make sure that...well...you know."

"And I appreciate it. Are you a neighbor?" I asked.

He nodded. "I'm Sonny. I live right across the street. I am the one who called for help."

"So, you found him?"

"Well not exactly," he said. "I heard the shot, but to be honest, it scared me so much I didn't dare to move. I fiddle with old cars for a hobby, antiques, so I was in my garage when I heard it. I didn't even look out the window; I just grabbed my phone and called 911. I told them I was certain I had heard a gunshot. I used to work at a gun range, so I knew exactly what I had heard. I waited for a while, scared out of my pants, then finally went into the kitchen and looked across the street. That's when I saw her drive out of the driveway and disappear. I wrote down the license plate and gave it to the sheriff when they got here. They told me she had just crashed and that they had her. I was so relieved that she wasn't out there anymore, hurting anyone else or coming for me, for that matter. It was terrifying."

"Had you seen her before?" I asked. "Had you seen her car around here before?"

He nodded. "Oh, yes. She came by a few days ago, and the car stayed in the driveway for several hours."

"Did they seem like they were arguing or fighting?" I asked.

"I wouldn't know about that. But that was the only other time I saw the car."

"What can you tell me about Harry Mayer? Did he have a lot of visitors? Was it unusual for him to have a visitor?"

"Oh, Harry never had anyone come by. He kept to himself lately. Ever since he was laid off."

"He was laid off? When did that happen?" I asked.

"Around three weeks ago. After that boy disappeared, the pastor's son. It was tough on him. He loved working with those horses."

"Horses? He worked for the Rutherfords?"

"You didn't know? He took care of their horses. They only have two, one for each of their spoiled kids."

I nodded, remembering seeing horses in the field behind their house. "But they have three children?" I said. "Shouldn't they have three horses then?"

Sonny smiled. "You'd think; wouldn't you?"

"What do you mean by that?"

Sonny shook his head. "Nothing. It's none of my business anyway. I gotta head back."

"Nice to meet you, Sonny, and thanks for the chat."

He smiled and nodded. "No problem, Detective."

I stared after him as he left, pondering his odd answer. It was the second time I had felt like there was something about the older brother, Charles Junior, that seemed out of place in that family. It wasn't like you couldn't ride horses when you were in a wheelchair; that was often something they could actually do and enjoy. Was he just not interested in riding? Why did I keep getting the feeling that he wasn't as adored as the other two? Or was there something else there I was missing?

I took one last glance around the living room, screening the area for things I might have missed when my eyes fell on a notepad on the end table next to the couch. I walked closer and picked it up. It looked like any ordinary notepad, except it wasn't. I had seen my friend Rebekka Franck with one exactly like it. As I stared at the words on it, I realized this wasn't Harry Mayer's notepad. This belonged to Eliza Reuben. She'd have to have left it here on one of her visits. I held it up to the light and could barely see what had been written on it. The pen had pressed through so hard it had left marks, and whatever had been on the page that was now ripped out also appeared on the page below. I used one of Harry's pencils to color over it, and soon the words stood out completely.

I rushed out to the car and Austin, then put the notepad in the back seat with a smile, feeling guilty. I wanted to spend some time with my son, and this had taken longer than expected.

"Okay. Let's go get us some donuts," I said as the car roared to life.

33

They were hammering on the sides of the trailer. Savannah stared at the door, her hands shaking. It had been going on all morning. Her mom had told her that they found the body of Benjamin in the creek the day before, and she had expected them to accuse her, but not this. Not them coming to her trailer and knocking on the sides of it, yelling at her.

"Killer!"

"Murderer!"

"Come on out and get your punishment!"

Savannah's mother held her in her arms while she waited for them to go away. Neither of them had dared to walk outside all morning, afraid of what the angry mob might do. Savannah was crying and hiding in her mother's embrace, wondering what she was going to do.

"They all think I killed him, Mom. How will I ever show my face anywhere again? How will I go to school?"

"You walk in there with your head lifted high, that's what you'll do. 'Cause you didn't do a darn thing."

"Can't I be homeschooled, please?" she asked. "I can't go there; I can't face those people. Why would they think that about me? Why would they believe that I murdered someone?"

"They don't know you, baby. They're just angry. They need someone to blame; that's all."

"But why me? Why would they pick me? Plenty of people could have killed Benjamin. Why me?"

Her mother swallowed, then looked into her daughter's eyes, tears springing to hers. "Because it's the easiest. Because you were there on the night it happened."

"But I wasn't the only one there. His family was there too. And Penny's boyfriend."

"I know, sweetie. It's awful, but you're the new kid. And you were the last one that people know saw him alive."

Savannah sighed and let her mother hold her tight, fearing for what was going to happen next when there was a knock on the door, sounding different from the banging they had heard all morning. Realizing that the yelling had stopped, Savannah lifted her head with a light gasp as another voice sounded from the outside.

"This is Sheriff Franklin; please, open the door."

Savannah's eyes met those of her mother, and she tried to smile to calm her daughter down, but it didn't work. Panic was stirring inside Savannah like a raging fire, and she wanted most of all to scream.

The knock came again accompanied by yelling.

"Open up!"

"I have to open it," her mother whispered, then let go of Savannah.

Savannah sobbed as her mother walked to the door, then glanced back at her one last second before turning the knob.

"Sheriff Franklin," she said.

His voice was heavy. "I need to talk to Savannah, ma'am. We're taking her in for questioning."

34

I was already awake when Shannon opened her eyes. She looked gorgeous in the light coming from outside the window, and part of me just wanted to stay in bed all day with her, doing nothing but staring at her, taking all of her in, every little part of her.

"Hey there," she said. "Have you been awake for long?"

I sighed and leaned over to kiss her. As our lips parted, I looked into her eyes. "Just a little while."

"It's getting to you, huh?"

"How can it not? Something is completely off. I am certain that Eliza Reuben didn't kill Harry Mayer, but the sheriff refuses to listen. I called them yesterday after going to his house, but they brushed me off. They won't even listen when I tell them I think she was just working on her story when she walked in on his dead body and that she tried to flee from the killer. They need to protect her out there at the hospital. The killer might be back to finish what he started."

"So, what do you think that this Harry Mayer told Eliza that was worth killing him for?" Shannon asked, looking up at me with her big eyes.

"That's what I really want to know. I asked Winston about her laptop when I called, but he said it was destroyed in the crash. They had sent it to a lab, trying to recover what was on it."

"So, let me get this straight. You think that Harry Mayer knew something about the murder of Benjamin Rutherford and that he told this to Eliza for her story and that's why he was killed?"

"Yes," I said, pensively. "I also think that the killer wanted to make it look like a suicide. That's why the gun was in his hand when Eliza came in and tried to revive him."

"And you also think that Lyle died because of this? That he also spoke to Eliza and that's why he was murdered?"

I sighed and closed my eyes briefly, then opened them again. "It was his name on the notepad. Someone had written his name down on the notepad, and I'm guessing he or she did it when she came on an earlier visit to Harry Mayer's house."

"So, you're assuming that Lyle must have known something too?" she asked. "But what could he have known? What's his link to the Rutherfords? Harry worked for them; we know that now, but what was Lyle's connection?"

I exhaled. "That's what I need to find out."

"And he couldn't just have committed suicide because he was carrying this knowledge and it was too much to bear?" Shannon asked.

"It's a possibility, yes, but why do it in front of someone's kid? Why risk someone finding out you have a gun when bringing it to a school filled with children? He could have done it at home. It just doesn't make sense. Plus, it was the exact same way Harry was placed, shot with a gun in his hand, like he had ended it himself, till Eliza came in. It can't be a coincidence. I just wish that Austin would talk to me and tell me what he saw, but he won't say a word."

I felt Shannon's hand on my arm. "He's scared, Jack. If you're right, then he witnessed a murder take place. We're lucky that he didn't get hurt too. If he saw who it was, then the killer could just as easily have shot him too, to shut him up."

"You're right," I said. "I didn't even think about that. He must have thought he was going to die. The boy's too terrified to tell. Maybe that's why he's still alive."

35

She was doing a little research of her own. Shannon had told Jack she was going downtown to grocery shop, which she would eventually, but she had a small errand to run first.

By snooping around on Instagram, she had learned that Benjamin had dated a girl named Colette before Savannah. She had found her on Instagram and messaged her.

Now, Shannon was looking for the small restaurant where Colette had said they could meet. It was located in a strip mall next to the main street, Soco Road.

Shannon parked in front of it, then reached over for her bag when she spotted someone else in the parking lot. At the end by the candy store stood two people, visibly in a heated argument.

Shannon wrinkled her nose and looked at them for a few seconds, wondering what was going on. Pastor Rutherford threw out his arms and gesticulated wildly, while the woman he spoke to wept. Seeing how agitated the pastor was, she grabbed her phone and took a couple of snapshots of the two of them, still observing them closely. The way the pastor was gesturing, it seemed like they were in a very intense debate, and he was the aggressive one. The woman—who Shannon had never seen before—cried and shook her bent-down head.

Is he going to hit her?

Having been in an abusive relationship for many years with Angela's father, Shannon knew the signs of a man who was capable of striking. It was the sudden movements, the anger in the eyes, and the built-up frustration that she could see in the way he moved and gestured. It made her heart start to race.

And just as she wondered what to do in case he lost it, it happened. The pastor lifted his hand in the air and let it fall on the cheek of this woman, slapping her. The woman let out a shriek, then fell sideways and held a hand to her cheek. Shannon felt her heart pound, then jumped out of the car, ready to defend this woman. But before she could, they had split up and were walking away from one another. Shannon rushed toward where they had been standing, but they were both gone. She turned around just in time to see the pastor rush out of the parking lot and roar past her, driving a black pick-up truck.

Shannon could hardly breathe as she saw it drive onto the street and disappear down the road. She grabbed her phone and wanted to call Jack, but then decided she could tell him this news later. She looked around to see if she could spot the woman anywhere, but she too was gone. She had probably taken the back road, Shannon thought, then spotted the small Italian restaurant that she was looking for squeezed in between a tile store on one side and a sandwich shop on the other. She looked at her watch and realized she was late, then rushed to the door and walked inside. She found a young girl looking a lot like the Instagram picture sitting at a table, then approached her.

"Colette?"

The girl smiled and stood up. "It really is you, then. I can't believe it. The famous Shannon King wants to hang out with me. I'm a huge fan. Whatever you want to know, I'll be happy to tell you."

Shannon exhaled. Sometimes, being famous had its advantages.

"Can I get you a soda or something?" she asked. "I, for one, need something to calm me down."

36

Maggie Valley 2018

They were doing great. Savannah had decided to let her concerns go and convinced herself that it was normal for Benjamin to be so close to his sister. After all, what did Savannah know about having a sibling? She had always been an only child. She had told Benjamin that she preferred it just to be the two of them when they dated, and that seemed to work out.

They had now been dating for about a year, and the people in town and at school had gotten used to thinking of them as a couple. The only ones that didn't seem to agree were their families. Especially his. It didn't matter how much Benjamin tried to hide it or brush her off when she mentioned it to him, but it was true. No one in his family liked her. It didn't matter how much she tried to please them; they barely looked at her or even spoke to her in more than a few short sentences, sometimes answering her questions with just one word.

It was very frustrating to her. Savannah couldn't for the life of her understand why they were so reluctant to accept her as part of their son's life. Was it because she didn't have a father? Was it because she lived in a trailer park? Was she simply not good enough for their precious son?

The thought made her sad, but it also made her even more determined to prove to them that she was nothing like they thought. She was so much more. She had big dreams for her future. Long ago, when her dad got sick, she had decided she wanted to go to med school. She wanted to help others like him; she wanted to be the one who saved the loved one of a family who needed him to stick around and couldn't live without him. That was what she thought about when she watched her dad be lowered into the ground at his funeral to the sound of her mother weeping. She wanted to be the doctor that prevented this from ever happening to another family.

It could have been avoided; the doctors had told them back then. If only Savannah's father had reacted when he started to feel the symptoms, they could have started treatment a lot earlier, and his chances would have been a lot better. But Savannah's dad had been coughing for years, and he had no time to be sick, so he ignored it and never saw a doctor till it was too late.

Savannah smiled and looked at Benjamin across the dining room table, while his mother served him potatoes, avoiding even asking if Savannah wanted some. She decided she didn't care about his family. It was him that she loved. It was him she wanted to be with, not them.

"Where's Penny?" his mother suddenly said.

It was Benjamin who had asked Savannah to stay for dinner, even though she didn't feel like it. He had told her the only way to win over his family's heart was to keep trying.

"They'll learn to love you eventually. They just need to warm up to you a little. Don't worry."

Those were his words, but they fell flat after having tried for an entire year.

"She's probably just out by the horses," Benjamin said and shoveled a couple more potatoes onto his plate, then served some to Savannah with a smile and a wink. "You know how she loves to hang out over there and often loses track of time."

"She knows when we're eating," the pastor said, speaking with his mouth full. "She should know to be here."

The front door slammed, and someone yelled from the hallway.

"I'm home."

Savannah swallowed her piece of chicken, then Benjamin slid his hand out of hers under the table and looked up at the sound of his sister's voice.

"Am I too late?" she said and stood in the doorway.

As Savannah laid her eyes on her, she almost choked on a piece of potato.

"Penelope, what on earth have you done to your hair?" her mother said. "Your beautiful blonde hair?"

Penelope smiled from ear to ear, then touched the tip of a brown lock. "I dyed it. Doesn't it look perfect? I look just like Savannah now; don't you think so, Benjamin? I posted a picture of it on Instagram, and a lot of people thought I was her. Isn't it pretty, Benji?"

37

It had snowed again the night before, and I took the kids out to play in it in the yard. We built a huge snowman and had a snowball fight. It felt so good to play around and not think about all that had happened since we got there for once. Even Austin seemed to be able to forget for a few seconds. He helped me get the head on top of the snowman and chuckled as half of it broke off on the way. I grumbled, annoyed, then gathered more snow and fixed the hole, patting it gently.

"He looks great; doesn't he?"

Austin bent down, then gathered a little more snow and placed it on top of the head, shaping a small hat.

"Now it's perfect, Dad."

Seeing my boy smile and play again made me so happy. I had realized all he needed was for me to let him off the hook for a little while and not keep pressuring him to talk about what had happened at the ski school. It wasn't easy since I wanted him to tell me; I desperately wanted to know what he had seen. It was beyond frustrating to know that he might have seen the killer but simply refused to talk about it. But we had been down that road, and it didn't lead us anywhere. He would talk when he was ready; Shannon had convinced me of that this morning in bed. For now, it was all about making the best of the time we had together.

Things hadn't exactly gone the way I wanted them to on this trip. By now, it was my plan that the kids would be so good at skiing that I would be able to take them up on the lift and ride down the green or maybe even red slopes with them. But that hadn't happened. So far, they had only had one day of ski school, and I wasn't sure I was ever going to get Austin back up there again.

"But it's missing something," I said.

"What, Dad?" Austin asked.

I pulled out an old pipe from my pocket that I had found inside the cabin and placed it in the mouth.

"There. Now it's perfect," I said and glanced at the other kids who were engaged in a huge snowball fight. I spotted Abigail as she gathered a snowball and ran after Tyler, then smashed it into his face with the result that Tyler let out a loud scream.

"Abigail!"

"What?" she yelled back. "He started it!"

While she was turned away, Tyler picked up a big chunk of snow, then walked to Abigail and slid it inside of her jacket. Abigail shrieked as the cold snow glided down her back. It was hard for me not to laugh.

"You little midget, I'm gonna get you," she screamed, then took off after Tyler.

Tyler squealed, then ran away, Abigail on his tail. Seconds later, they ended up on the neighbor's property and kept going.

"Hey, you two, come back here."

They disappeared around the neighbor's house, and soon I couldn't see them anymore.

"Hey, guys! Come back here. It's not our property over there."

I exchanged a glance first with Betsy Sue, then Angela, and finally Austin.

"Where did they go?" I asked.

Austin shrugged. We waited for a few seconds more before I exhaled.

"Guess I'll have to go get them. Go ahead and go inside. I'll be right back."

38

"I don't like to talk about him much."

Colette sipped her Sprite, distraught, her eyes avoiding Shannon's. They had ordered two pasta dishes, and now she was nibbling breadsticks while they waited.

"And why is that?" Shannon asked. "Why don't you like to talk about Benjamin?"

"Oh, it's not because of him. It's just, well...it wasn't for me."

"Was it because of his sister?" Shannon asked. "His brother mentioned that she was part of the reason why you broke up with him."

"Not part. She was all the reason. I liked Benjamin. He was cute and very considerate. But his sister was nuts if you ask me."

Colette grabbed a breadstick and took a bite.

"Tell me about her. What was so nuts about her?" Shannon asked, glancing briefly at her phone. There had been no calls; the kids were probably fine.

"Pretty much everything. She would never leave us alone. She went with us everywhere we went—the movies, restaurants, everywhere. If I was snuggling with Benjamin on the couch, she would crawl up to him from the other side and lay really close to him like she was his darn girlfriend. She would often say that she could never find a boyfriend as good as her brother. It felt like they were the ones dating and not him and me. I got the feeling she wanted to be with him, which grossed me out."

"So, they were close? Some siblings are closer than others."

Colette shook her head. "No, it was more than that. It was like she was in love with him. And she was constantly trying to get me out of the way. She'd ignore me and hardly talk to me, or she'd text him when he was with me and write that he didn't need to be with me anymore, not when he had her. I only dated him for five months before I had enough of her. She was so creepy the way she watched us when we were watching TV at his house or how I would see her in the window when kissing him goodnight on the porch. I was scared of her, to be honest. I didn't feel safe."

Shannon chewed the breadstick, then the pasta arrived, and she dug in, starving. All this cold air made her hungry. Colette put her fork into her pasta, then paused and dropped the fork back on the plate.

"I've never told anyone this before, but I think she attacked me once."

Shannon almost choked on her pasta and drank a sip of her water. "She attacked you? What do you mean you *think* she attacked you?"

"I couldn't really see that it was her. She was wearing a ski mask. I was walking home one night after watching a movie with some friends. I had parked in the back behind the movie theater and, as I said goodbye to my friends and walked to my car, someone jumped me from behind. A hand was placed over my mouth so I couldn't scream, and as I fought to get loose from this person's grip, I saw the watch the person was wearing on their arm. I took a self-defense class a couple of months earlier, so I managed to use that to get away, and the person ran off. At the time, I thought it was some random guy, and I never told anyone since nothing really happened and my mother didn't know I was out so late. She works nights at a nursing home outside of town, so I'm often out later than my curfew without her knowing it. But the next time I was at Benjamin's house, I saw Penny wearing that same watch. That's actually why I broke up with him. I told him I thought his sister attacked me, and he refused to believe me. He said I was jealous of her and that was it. I'd had enough."

"Wow," Shannon said and ate the last of her pasta, then looked at the girl across from her.

"I'm just glad I got away from that family. That sister is terrifying. Now that Benjamin is dead, I feel so sad, but to be honest, I'm not that surprised. I'm certain his sister killed him because she knew she could never have him, and she couldn't bear that someone else would."

39

"Abigail? Tyler?"

I ran across the heavy snow, around the big house next door, following their footsteps, but still, I couldn't see them. I looked up at the big house, hoping the Rutherfords wouldn't see us out here and get angry at us for trespassing. They were still grieving the loss of their son, and I wouldn't want to interrupt or make them feel uncomfortable.

"Abigail and Tyler. You come back here, now!"

A couple of horses made sounds from the field at the end of the property where they had a small stable, but I couldn't see the kids anywhere down there either. I turned to see their footsteps leading to the other end of the property, then decided to follow them. They led me to a small shack very close to the creek.

I called their names again, but they didn't answer, and now I could see their footprints leading to the back door of the shack. They must have run inside. Tyler was probably trying to hide from his sister in there, and so she had followed.

I walked to the door, then pushed it open gently. "Tyler? Abigail? Hello? Are you in there?"

A sound made me go in. The room was like a shed with a ton of garden equipment and bags of food for the horses. I spotted both kids at the end of the room. They were standing in the darkness, looking at something.

"There you are," I said, relieved, but beginning to get cross with them for running away like that.

Neither of them moved as I spoke. They stood like statues and stared at an old freezer, holding the lid open.

"What are you doing?" I asked angrily. It was one thing to run in somewhere by accident because they were goofing around, but snooping in other people's things wasn't okay.

"You've got to see this, Dad," Abigail said and pointed.

I approached the freezer, then looked down into it. Blood was smeared on the inside.

"W-what is that, Dad?" Tyler asked, barely able to look inside unless he stood on his tippy toes. Abigail was holding the lid.

I exhaled and stared at the blood.

"Tyler looked inside because he wanted to hide inside of it," Abigail said when she saw my expression. "He lifted the lid and then he saw the blood. It wasn't me."

I grabbed Tyler's hand in mine and pulled him away. "Don't you ever try to crawl into a freezer to hide, you hear me? Some of these old ones can't open from the inside, and you'll freeze to death. Now, let's get out of here. We're trespassing."

Abigail grabbed my other hand. "What do you think was in there? Where did all the blood come from?"

I exhaled, then took a picture of it with my phone. "I don't know, sweetie. Now, let's go."

As we approached the door, we heard the sound of footsteps creaking on the snow outside, and soon a man stood in front of us.

"What are you doing here?" he asked.

"My kids were playing around. They ran in here by mistake," I said. "We've rented the cabin next door for the week. Who are you?"

"I'm Douglas Rutherford. I'm Charles' brother. I'm staying here while I wait for my wife to figure out if she wants to divorce me or not."

As he spoke, I realized his breath reeked of alcohol, and he was swaying slightly. I smiled politely, then walked past him into the snow.

"I'm sorry for the inconvenience. As I said, they ran in here by mistake. We'll just head back now."

As I walked past him, holding my kids close, I felt his eyes follow us all the way back to our cabin, and it made the hairs rise on the back of my neck. As soon as I reached our place, I grabbed my phone and called the sheriff.

40

"So, you're telling me you saw the pastor in a fight with some woman downtown?"

Jack stared at Shannon, his eyes wide. She was unpacking the groceries when she told him what she had seen. She put away the lamb she had bought for tonight, then reached for her phone and showed him the picture of them together that she had taken from inside the car.

"They were discussing something, and he got aggressive. Finally, he slapped her, and then she left. It almost made me call the cops, but then they were gone, and I didn't know what to do."

Jack stared at the display. "Wow. That's awful. He really hit her? I can't believe it. Do you know who the woman is?"

"No," Shannon said as she found a pack of Oreos and put them on a shelf. "But it's strange, right?"

"Sure is," he said, wrinkling his forehead. "And you say he drove away in a black pick-up truck? Did you recognize it as the same one that we saw that day?"

She shrugged. "Black pick-up trucks are pretty common around here. But it did make me wonder."

Jack exhaled. "Something is not right over there; I can tell you that much. The kids accidentally ran onto the neighbor's property today. They were goofing around and didn't realize they were trespassing. Tyler and Abigail got themselves into an old shack in the back where they found a freezer. And get this; it had blood smeared inside of it."

Shannon dropped the bag of sliced bread onto the counter. She turned to look at him.

"You're kidding me? Real blood?"

Jack shook his head. "It looked like it, yes. There was nothing in it now, but I couldn't help wondering..."

"You think someone kept Benjamin's body in there, don't you? Until it was released into the water."

He sighed. "I don't know. But it's a possibility, right? I mean it's been three weeks since he disappeared, and then suddenly out of the blue, he turns up in the creek? His body is barely decomposed. A body that has been in the water for a long time shows sign of having been in there. Usually, there's scavenging, but there was nothing to see on him. Nothing at all."

Shannon nodded. "It does sound strange. Okay, let's say he was in the freezer for all this time; who put him there?"

"I don't know. We met his uncle who, apparently, stays in the small shack while waiting for a divorce. I thought about asking him about the blood, just to see his reaction or maybe find out if there was a logical explanation for it; maybe they had shot a deer and kept it in there or something, but to be honest, I didn't feel comfortable around him. He reeked of alcohol and could barely stand up straight. I rushed out of there with the children instead."

"So, he could have killed him and kept him there," she said. "It would be obvious since he lives there. But what about his sister, Penny? She attacked his ex-girlfriend, and according to the older brother, she's the reason that Savannah broke up with him. Could she have killed her own brother and kept him in that freezer?"

Jack shuddered at the thought while Shannon put the cheese in the fridge. She had told him everything about her meeting with both Charles and Colette. Jack didn't like that she was snooping around on her own, he said, but she got the feeling that he was impressed with her, even though he didn't want to show it.

"It's possible," he said. "If she's as obsessed with her brother as you were told, then it sounds like Penny has serious psychological problems."

"And you think all of this is somehow connected to Eliza Reuben's crash too, right? That she knew something and was writing a story about it and that this Harry Mayer and Lyle Bishop were her sources, even though we don't know Lyle's connection to the Rutherfords yet. We do know she wrote his name on her notepad, right?" Shannon asked, trying to keep track of the story. It was beginning to get quite complicated.

Jack nodded when his phone vibrated, and he picked it up, then walked outside on the porch to make sure he wasn't disturbed by the children. A few minutes later, he returned.

"That was the medical examiner," he said. "I called in a favor with an old colleague of mine and had him answer a few questions about Lyle Bishop's autopsy."

"And?"

"His hand was broken. Lyle's right hand was broken at the time he died, the same hand the gun was found in. It's pretty hard to shoot yourself with a broken hand. That also tells me someone forced his hand, maybe by turning the gun toward himself, trying to make it look like he did it to himself."

"And no matter how you look at it, it doesn't look much like suicide anymore," Shannon said. "The texts to his friends and family could have been sent by the killer after Lyle was dead. I think you're on to something, Jack. You should talk to the sheriff about this. Tell him your theory."

Jack shook his head. "I tried earlier today. I called and told them that I thought Eliza was running from the killer when she crashed and that I believed she was still in danger."

"Let me guess; they didn't believe you?"

"The sheriff didn't say so in words, but that was the feeling I got. He simply told me that they had this under control and Eliza had a guard by her door, so there was nothing to worry about. I called again later and told them about the freezer, and they said they'd come have a look at it, but so far, they haven't been here." Jack glanced out the window, then paused. "I think I'll go over there and greet them when they do get here," he said and grabbed his coat and boots.

"I'll make us all some hot chocolate when you come back in. I bought marshmallows too."

"That sounds absolutely wonderful," Jack said, and he leaned over the counter and kissed her before he disappeared out the door and let a blast of freezing wind in.

As Shannon turned around and looked out the window toward the house next door, she was certain she saw the young girl standing in the window, staring down at her.

41

Maggie Valley 2018

"I don't want you to see her anymore."

The words fell in the kitchen of Benjamin's house. Savannah felt completely paralyzed when she heard it. She couldn't believe her own ears. The words came from Benjamin's mother. She had pulled him aside just as the two of them walked into the hallway after having been out for a drive. It had been a beautiful summer evening, and they had watched the sun set behind the mountains while kissing inside the car. As they drove back, she had felt like she was floating on a cloud of happiness. It was hard for Savannah to admit, but she was in love with Benjamin, and tonight had sealed the deal for her. He had given her a necklace with a cute heart on it.

But now she had come down from her cloud. Benjamin's mother spoke like Savannah wasn't standing right behind him. She almost spoke like she wasn't a person at all...like she wasn't someone she knew and had known for a year now. Savannah had been having dinners at their house; she had been spending evening after evening in their living room, watching movies or sitting on the porch and talking to Benjamin. She knew they didn't like her much, but this? This, she had never expected from them.

"What the heck?" Benjamin said. "That's not something you get to decide. I am seventeen, for crying out loud. You don't decide who I date and who I don't date."

"Yes, we do. Your dad and I agree. This relationship isn't good for you. We want you to stop seeing her. You can argue all you want. It's not up for negotiation."

"It's because of her, isn't it?" Benjamin asked with a snort. "It's all because of her."

"I don't know what you're talking about," his mother replied. "And I don't want to talk to you about it anymore. There's nothing you can say or do to make us change our minds. The decision is made."

"But why?"

"Just do as you're told, Benjamin," his mother said, turning away from him to continue peeling potatoes. "As long as you live under our roof, you obey our rules."

"I can't believe you!"

Benjamin turned around and looked at Savannah, then grabbed her hand and pulled her out onto the porch. He took her face between his hands and looked her in the eyes. "I am so sorry about that. I am not going to let them ruin what we have. I love you, Savannah. I have never felt this way about any other girl."

Savannah felt like crying but held it back. She felt helpless. What were they going to do?

"But...she said that..."

"Sh," he said. "Don't listen to her. She doesn't have to know. Neither does my dad."

"But...but how?"

"There are ways, Savannah. I'll find ways for us to be together. I'll turn eighteen in less than a year, and then we can run away. I'm not letting them destroy us; I am not letting them come between us, you hear me?"

"You know my mom doesn't like me seeing you either," she said.

"She's said so from the beginning that she didn't want me to see you. I've done so anyway, but we can't be at my place either."

"Then we'll hang in the car. We'll see movies and take drives to the countryside. We'll be together, Savannah, I promise you we will."

Savannah looked into his eyes, searching for comfort. This news had devastated her. Up until now, they had spent most of their time at his house. How were they going to be with one another in this small town without their parents knowing? It seemed impossible.

"What did you mean by what you said to your mother?" she asked. "You said that it was because of her. What did you mean by that?"

Benjamin smiled and kissed her. "Don't worry about it," he said, as their lips parted.

"You meant Penny, didn't you? She's the one who has been trying to stop us from seeing each other, right?"

"As I said, you don't have to worry about it," he said. "Everything is going to be fine. I've got this under control."

"I'm just... She scares me, Benjamin."

He kissed her again. "Relax. We'll find a way to be together. Trust me on this."

She swallowed, then nodded. They heard footsteps coming up behind them and turned to see Penny standing on the porch. It was dark, so Savannah could barely see her eyes, but she felt them on her skin like knives.

"She's not supposed to be here," Penny said. "Mom and Dad don't want her here anymore."

"Savannah is just leaving," Benjamin said. "You don't have to keep a constant eye on me. Go back inside."

But Penny stayed where she was. She didn't move one inch. She stood by the window, and as the light from inside hit her neck, Savannah noticed something around her neck. As she squinted her eyes, she realized she was staring at a necklace exactly the same as the one Benjamin had given her.

Seeing it made Savannah feel like she had to throw up.

She looked at him. "What's going on here, Benjamin? Did you give her a necklace too?"

He exhaled. "I had to. She was with me when I bought it, and she freaked out that I was going to buy you a necklace and not her. She kept pleading with me to buy her one as well. Does it really matter?"

Savannah pulled away from him, tears welling up in her eyes. "Yes, it matters. It matters a great deal. I thought you bought this especially for me because I meant something to you. And then I find out that you...you bought one for your sister too? Just because you can't say no to her? That's sick, Benjamin."

She pulled the necklace off and handed it to him.

"Here. I don't want it."

"Savannah...please, don't be..."

But it was too late. Savannah had turned around and was running to her car. She got in and, as she started the engine, she was certain she saw Penny laugh as her face was lit up by the light from the window next to her.

PART III

42

"Come on, Savannah. Just tell us the truth. You got mad at him, didn't you? It's perfectly understandable if you did. He was being an idiot, a bastard, and you hit him with something. Was it a baseball bat? Or a garden tool that was left out on the porch?"

Sheriff Franklin sat across the table from Savannah. They had kept her inside this small room for hours, and she was so tired of having to say the same thing again and again.

"I didn't hurt him. I swear; I didn't."

"But you broke up with him."

"Since when is that a crime?" she asked, feeling exhausted. "Yes, I told him I didn't want to see him anymore."

"And you're sure it wasn't the other way around?"

"You mean am I sure that I broke up with him and not him breaking up with me? Yes, I am sure."

"Did him breaking up with you make you mad?" he asked.

Savannah shook her head. The sheriff leaned back in his chair that seemed way too small for such a big man. His khaki shirt was a size too small on his stomach, and it looked like the buttons would pop at any second now.

"He didn't break up with me. I broke up with him. I don't know what happened to him afterward. I drove home. I've told you this a million times." Savannah hid her face between her hands. She was so tired. It seemed like this nightmare would never stop.

"His parents were against you two seeing one another, am I right?"

Savannah nodded. "They had told him never to see me again. But that was a few months earlier."

"And your mother was against it too, but you were still dating?" he asked. "How come?"

"We loved one another. My mother had been against us from the beginning. She told me he was trouble, that someday I would regret it."

"But you did it anyway?"

"Well, yes. She didn't like it much, but I told her I couldn't choose who I loved. I loved him, and there was nothing she could do to stop me from dating him. I think she learned to look the other way."

"But Benjamin's parents weren't like that, were they?" the sheriff asked.

Savannah shook her head, remembering the conversation in the kitchen with Benjamin's mother. It had broken her heart that they could be so cruel. How could they be so cold toward her and their own son?

"No. They forbade him to see me at one point. His mother told him while I was there one day."

"Yet, you were at his house on the day he disappeared?"

Savannah bit her lip. "Yeah, well, for a while we kept it a secret that we were still seeing one another. We would sneak around and just go places in his brother's truck. Well, it was mostly Benjamin's truck now that Charles couldn't drive anymore. But one day a couple of months later, he told me things had changed. His mother had agreed to let me come back to his house again...that they weren't against us dating anymore."

Sheriff Franklin looked up from his papers. His eyes narrowed. "What changed?"

Savannah shrugged. "I don't know. He never told me. But the next time I went there, his mother didn't say anything. She just nodded at me, then went upstairs. I never knew why she changed her mind or what made her resent me in the first place."

The door to the interrogation room opened, and a deputy peeked inside. "Sheriff, you're needed."

Sheriff Franklin exhaled and got up from his chair with much trouble. "We're not done here, young lady, but I'll let you rest for a little while. We're keeping you here, though. Not just for interrogation, but also for your own protection. There's still a mob gathered outside, waiting to get their hands on you."

43

"This better be good, Ryder. For dragging me all the way out here again and bothering this family."

Sheriff Franklin gave me a look that made me feel like a child having troubled his parents in the middle of an important conversation.

"It is," I said. "I think you'll find this to be more than interesting."

Deputy Winston had been the first one to arrive, and he was now on the porch talking to the pastor, who was gesticulating wildly, while I spoke to the sheriff.

"What are you talking about?" the pastor yelled. "I don't see why..."

Sheriff Franklin sighed heavily.

"Let's get this over with as fast as humanly possible," he said and looked up at the pastor, then back at me. "I had Judge Williams give us a warrant before I left, so he can yell all he wants to. But there better be something, Ryder."

"It was in the shack down there," I said and pointed toward the small house by the creek. "The back door led into a room with garden tools and an old freezer. My kids ran in there by accident trying to play hide-and-seek, and that's when they saw the blood."

Sheriff Franklin nodded, then signaled for his other deputy to follow him. "Okay. We'll go have a look."

The pastor had stopped yelling and was now glaring at them as they strode up through the snow toward the shack, me leading the way. I reached the door from earlier, then pushed it open.

"Over there by the end wall," I said and pointed. "That's the freezer."

Sheriff Franklin stepped in with a sniffle and pulled up his pants before he reached the freezer. A deputy handed him a glove, and he lifted the lid, then paused. He turned to look at me.

"You mind coming here for a second?"

I walked closer, sensing something was off. I looked inside the freezer and realized it was completely clean.

"I...It can't be...wait," I said and reached inside my pocket. I pulled out my phone and found the picture I had taken earlier, then showed it to him.

"This was how it looked a few hours ago. My guess is someone cleaned the freezer."

The sheriff felt the side with his finger and sniffed. "Does smell like it was recently cleaned."

"The uncle who lives in this shack saw us come out of here earlier. He could easily have cleaned it out."

Sheriff Franklin scratched his forehead under the hat. "I don't know what to say, Ryder. Even if the blood was there like I can see in your picture it was, then it could have been from some animal they kept here from hunting or some meat that spilled, or maybe it wasn't even blood at all. I guess now we'll never know."

I exhaled, annoyed. If the blood had still been there, they could at least have it analyzed, and then we'd know if it belonged to Benjamin or not.

"We found something," one of the deputies said from the other end of the room. "Sheriff?"

Sheriff Franklin turned, and I followed him closely as he strode across the floor. The deputy had found a hatch in the floor and opened it. He reached inside and pulled out a fire poker. It was covered in blood.

44

Shannon watched from the window, eating Oreos from the box. The kids were playing upstairs, making an awful noise, but at least they were having fun, except for Austin, who was sitting by the fireplace, drawing. Shannon glanced at him and felt terrible. He was such a sensitive kid.

As she grabbed another Oreo, Shannon saw someone come up to the front door and knock. She recognized her as Bridget Westwood, the hostess at Joey's Pancake House and owner of their cabin. Jack had told her that she owned a couple of cabins in the area that she rented out and made a living from, while she lived a couple of blocks down the street with her husband and two dogs.

Shannon opened the door. "Hello, Mrs. Westwood."

"I am terribly sorry to interrupt, but I need a check for the last two days. Jack originally only booked the cabin for four days but then wrote me and told me he wanted to stay six days in total. He said he would pay me when he got here."

"Of course. I'm so sorry that he hasn't done so already," Shannon said and let Bridget inside. She glanced at the neighboring house and the police activity then walked in and closed the door behind her. She smiled and waved at Austin, who looked up as she entered.

"Cute kid."

"Thanks," Shannon said, even though she had nothing to do with the creation of Austin. She still saw him as her own. Shannon grabbed her checkbook from her purse and started to write.

"Say, you wouldn't happen to know what's going on at the Rutherfords', would you?" Bridget asked and peeked out the window.

Shannon shook her head. She remembered that Jack had told her to be careful what she told Bridget since she liked to gossip. "I think they're examining the place; you know...combing through it for evidence and such. I don't know, really."

"Really? They must have found something since there are so many cars and even a van from the county. It belongs to the crime scene techs."

"I guess they must have found something then," Shannon said and handed the woman the check. She took it while scrutinizing Shannon. It made her feel a little uncomfortable.

"It's all very strange what's going on around here lately. Makes one wonder, doesn't it? Did you hear about what happened to the Bishops' son?"

"Lyle?" Shannon said and glanced at Austin. She didn't want him to hear that they were talking about Lyle.

"Sure. We heard."

Mrs. Westwood shook her head. "Terrible ordeal. I think he killed himself because he knew what happen that night that Benjamin disappeared. He was there, you know? He was in the house that night. I'm beginning to think he might have seen something."

Shannon stared at the woman in front of her. "He was there? Why was he at the Rutherfords' house?"

"You didn't know? Lyle dated the daughter, Penelope. Come to think of it, that might also be why he killed himself. The girl never gave him the time of day. It's so sad, though. He was handsome and sweet too."

Shannon hardly blinked. They had been searching for Lyle's connection to the family, and there it was. Of course, Bridget knew this. They should have thought about asking her before.

She reached into her pocket and found the picture she had taken that same morning and showed it to Bridget.

"Do you know who that is?"

"That's the pastor...and the one he's talking to? Well, that's Susan Kelsey, Savannah's mother."

"Savannah...as in the girl that dated Benjamin?"

"Yes, that's the one. I wonder what they were talking about. Looks quite agitated, don't you think?"

45

The gin burned in his throat, yet he kept drinking it. The bottle was on his lips, and he refused to take it away. He needed the gin; he needed it to get rid of all the thoughts rumbling around inside of him.

Douglas breathed through his nose as he emptied the bottle before putting it down. He then gasped for air and leaned on the back of the old couch in the shack where his brother had let him stay.

Douglas coughed as the burning sensation subsided. It didn't help, he realized. The gin hadn't managed to drown it out, this nagging feeling that tormented him.

Usually, at this time of day, he was able to drink enough to doze off completely, but not today. Was it because the police were crawling all over the place, rummaging in the back?

They had been inside his small space and asked him about the freezer, but Doug had told them he knew nothing about it and then given them the old story about him only living there while waiting to see if his wife wanted to divorce him. Truth was, he had received the divorce papers months ago, but he just refused to sign them. They just lay there on the dresser, staring back at him, mocking him for what he had become.

I am sorry, Ginger. I am so terribly sorry. I just don't know how to stop. I don't know how to go back.

He had slapped her back in New York, where they had shared a beautiful old loft. Both of them were artists. She was a writer, and he was a painter. This meant they were both home all day, each working on their projects. But she was the one with success, not Douglas. He couldn't sell a painting even if his life depended on it, and sometimes it felt like it did.

Meanwhile, she had gotten a deal with a big publishing house, and her books were printed in sixteen countries around the world. It was her money that paid for the loft and everything else in their life. And he didn't even have a penny to his name. It was old-fashioned to be thinking that way, but maybe he was just that. He didn't like it one bit that he couldn't even contribute.

So, as the rejection letters kept coming from exhibitions and galleries, he soon took to drinking and didn't look back. He had hardly painted anything for almost a year now. Not since she threw him out and told him not to come back. How could he? She was his muse. There was no reason for him to paint anymore. Not without her in his life.

Douglas finally felt the buzz as the alcohol took over and the world spun around him. He couldn't stop thinking about that night three weeks ago and had to clutch onto the armrest to keep his hands from shaking. He sat like that for a few minutes, wondering if he should just go back there and tell them the truth, tell them what had happened. He couldn't stand the guilt he was feeling. It didn't matter if he was sent to jail for what he had done. Nothing mattered anymore.

Douglas pushed himself to an upright position when he realized he was in no condition to be moving around. He was so dizzy that he had to sit back down right away in order not to fall.

Douglas chuckled, but soon it turned to sobbing at how pathetic he had become. Seconds later, he was sound asleep on the flower-patterned couch. When he woke up again, the police had finished and left. It was quiet in his small shack again.

Except for the sound of footsteps approaching, walking slowly across the wooden planks.

46

"What happened over there?"

Shannon had served me some hot chocolate, and I was warming my fingers on the sides of the cup. I had been gone all afternoon and darkness had settled outside. My nose was so cold I could hardly feel it after spending hours at the neighboring house, while the sheriff and his team searched the shack.

"They found what they believe is the murder weapon," I said victoriously. Now, there was no longer any talk about suicide or Benjamin slipping and hurting his head on a rock in the creek. Now they were certain they were talking murder.

"It was a fire poker. It still had blood on it. Doesn't take a genius to see that it was what was used to hit Benjamin on the back of his head before he ended up in the freezer and then later in the creek."

Shannon wrinkled her nose. "Creepy."

I sipped my cup and felt the liquid as it spread warmth throughout my body, and I slowly came back to myself. I wasn't used to this kind of cold. Having lived all my life in Florida, this was very different, and not quite as romantic as I wanted it to be.

"But that's good news, right?" Shannon said and put an extra marshmallow in my cup with a smile. She knew how much I loved those. "That they found the weapon?"

"That is very good news. Now, they can check the poker for any fingerprints or DNA."

"So, maybe they'll catch the killer, then?" Shannon asked and put a dish in the dishwasher. The counter was smeared with leftover chocolate and cookie crumbs, and I realized I had missed out on quite the party. Now, the kids were watching a movie in the living room with the fireplace going.

"But someone cleaned the freezer, you say?" she asked and wiped the counter for crumbs.

"Yes, it was completely cleansed, not a drop of blood to be found inside of it. Luckily, I had the picture."

"That must mean that whoever is behind this must have known that you were in the shack."

"That's what I was thinking too. There was the uncle, who we met outside when we came out. He seemed a little off. I hope they bring him in for questioning."

Shannon smiled and closed the dishwasher. She reached over and grabbed my hand in hers. She looked me in the eyes with a deep sigh.

"How about we let go of all this for tonight? Listen to that. The kids are laughing at the movie. How about we join them and forget the world outside for a few hours, huh? Just be a family for once. The children miss us; they miss being with us, and that was kind of the idea with this vacation. For all of us to spend time together."

I exhaled, exhausted, then finished my hot chocolate. "That is the best idea I have heard all week."

We walked to the kids who were watching *The Incredibles 2*, then plunged down onto the couch together. Abigail crawled into my lap, and a few minutes later, I was snoring lightly with my daughter on top of me, Elastigirl doing her thing on the screen, while I was far away in the land of my dreams.

We had made it about halfway through the movie when I was awakened by a loud scream.

"What was that?" I asked, shooting upright with a confused grunt, sleepiness still lingering in my eyes. At first, I believed it was part of my dream, but as my eyes met Shannon's and I saw the concern in them, I knew it wasn't.

"It came from the neighbors," she said.

47

He made it outside. His perpetrator was close behind him, breathing down his neck. Douglas felt like it was all still a dream. It had such a dreamlike feel to it; the footsteps approaching inside the shack, the gun he had seen in the hand of the person coming for him. The sight had sobered him up immediately, yet the alcohol in his blood had still made it hard for him to see straight and to run. But he had tried anyway. Realizing that this person wanted to kill him, he had jumped out the window, through the glass, and cut himself on the arm and leg, but landed softly in the snow outside before rolling down the hill toward the creek. The perpetrator had been in the light of the window as he looked back up, then run for the door. Meanwhile, he had gotten back on his feet, but as he stood up, he slipped on the wet rocks and hurt his jaw. Now as he was running in the ice-cold water, he tasted blood in his mouth.

It had gotten dark out, which was to his advantage, but his perpetrator had a flashlight, and he could see its beam as it searched for him in between the tall trees and along the creek. The water was crackling loudly beneath him, and Douglas knew it well enough to know that if he stayed close to the banks, the water was shallow, and he could avoid falling in.

Douglas panted as he jumped from rock to rock in the darkness, hoping and praying he wouldn't fall. Behind him, he could hear his follower as they got closer still. Douglas cursed himself for drinking so much that it was hard for him to run. The many years of drinking had taken its toll on his body. He used to be in such good shape, but that was all gone.

Come on, Doug. You can make it. You were the fastest track runner in your senior year.

The beam from the flashlight fell on his shoulder, and Doug gasped. Then a shot was fired, and it echoed through the trees. Heart pounding in his throat, Doug ducked down, and the bullet whistled past him. He landed on all fours in the water, and his pants got soaked.

He stayed down for a few seconds, while his heart pounded against his ribcage. He gasped to breathe properly and rose to his feet. He ran forward, jumping two more rocks ahead before he slipped once again on a rock and landed face-first in the water, hitting his shin on the rock. Douglas shrieked in pain and felt his leg. Blood was gushing out from it. He thought he could feel the bone where there used to be skin. He had split his shin once before when jumping in a pool in Florida and hitting it on the edge. It took eight stitches done by the local mayor who was also a doctor.

Oh, dear God, I'll probably need to get to a hospital and have this stitched.

Douglas heard steps coming up behind him and a rustle between the bushes and realized his perpetrator was gaining on him. Doug stood to his feet but couldn't put any weight on his leg. He tried to jump forward using just one leg as he heard the person closing in and the gun being cocked again right behind his head.

Douglas fell forward and landed with both his hands on the rocks, covered in water, crying.

"Please. You don't have to do this."

"Oh, yes, Douglas, I do."

"Why? Why are you doing this to me?"

"You know why," the voice said, hissing. "You know perfectly well why I am doing this, you pathetic excuse for a human being."

"I didn't do anything," he said, sobbing. "I didn't tell. I promise; I didn't tell anyone. When the police questioned me, I told them I hadn't seen anything that night. I said I was drunk on my couch and that I didn't know anything. That's all. I promise; I didn't tell."

"But you told someone else," the voice said. "Didn't you? If you think it over really carefully, I'm sure you'll know what I'm talking about."

Douglas felt confused. He didn't remember saying anything, ever, but as he lay there in the water, feeling pathetic and soaked, a gun to his head, he suddenly remembered.

"The woman," he said. "At the bar. She came to me, and she...we talked...and..."

"And you were so drunk that you couldn't stop talking. Even though you knew you had to keep quiet, that everything depended on you keeping your big fat mouth shut. But that woman was a very well-known reporter. And you just handed her the story on a silver platter. That's how she came up with the idea. By talking to you, you fool. You're the one who led her to us. You're the reason it all went wrong."

Douglas could hardly breathe. It was true. He hadn't remembered until now because he had been so wasted, but yes, he now remembered vaguely talking about that night with some woman at the Legends Sports Grill downtown. He had told her about what had happened, hadn't he? He had told her everything—every freaking ugly detail.

"Oh, dear God," he mumbled.

"That's right, Douglas. You better pray that God will have mercy on your ugly sinful soul. 'Cause the way I see it, you're going straight to hell for what you've done."

"I am so sorry. I am so sorry..." Douglas cried and pleaded, but he knew it was in vain. Suddenly, he regretted everything in his life. He regretted having ever taken a drink; he regretted having left Ginger and New York and feeling sorry for himself for not being able to make a living. At least he had a woman who loved him, at least she could pay for him to follow his passion. What had been so bad about that? And why hadn't he stopped drinking when she asked—no pleaded with him to? Why had he been such a fool all his life? Why had he been such a coward?

"I'm..."

"It's too late for sorry," the voice said, and Douglas felt the gun press against his hair in the back.

Douglas closed his eyes when he felt the rippling water push his hand, and he slipped and slid to the side. The water was pulling at him forcefully, and he swallowed, waiting for his death when a thought struck him like lightning from a clear blue sky.

Why not give it a try? What can you possibly have to lose?

He then grabbed a rock with both hands and used it to push himself into the freezing water, just as the gun went off behind him.

48

I grabbed my coat and boots again, and Shannon gave me a flashlight, so I could find my way as I walked outside. As soon as I was on the porch, I felt the biting cold on my cheeks, and suddenly I longed terribly for those nights in Florida where the warmth felt like a blanket around you, and you could hear the cicadas everywhere you went.

I didn't need the flashlight much, though, since the area in front of the neighbor's house was lit up by red and blue blinking lights from the many police cruisers parked in the driveway.

"What's going on?" I mumbled to myself, then rushed toward the house, walking in the thick snow. As I approached it, I soon paused. The door was open, and now I saw two deputies as they came out. Between them, they were holding someone, dragging her kicking and screaming out on the porch. Behind her, someone else screamed too, and my heart sank.

"NO! she's my daughter. You can't take my daughter away from me!"

Mrs. Rutherford tried to yank one of the deputy's shoulders, but Sheriff Franklin pulled her back. As her daughter was dragged away,

Mrs. Rutherford fell to her knees on the porch, hiding her face between her hands.

"Please."

Sheriff Franklin came up behind her and placed a hand on her shoulder. I could see the pastor and Charles Junior behind them, a startled and shocked look on their faces while Penny was being put in the cruiser by the two deputies.

"I am sorry," Sheriff Franklin said, "that it has come to this, but as I said, her fingerprints were on the fire poker. Just her fingerprints and no one else's."

The blazing wind carried his words toward me, and as I heard them, my heart stopped. I couldn't believe it. Penny had killed her brother? From inside the cruiser, I could hear her violent screams as the cruiser took off, driving into the darkness, sirens blaring, blinking lights turning the night a gloomy blue. Sheriff Franklin put on his hat and followed them in his cruiser, leaving the grieving family on the porch.

I turned to look at Mrs. Rutherford, still on her knees on the wooden planks as she sobbed and pleaded for her daughter, for them to have mercy on her when the pastor spotted me standing beside the house.

"You!" he almost screamed. He rushed toward me, down the stairs so fast I barely managed to move away. He was soon in my face, his hands on my throat, pressing me backward till I hit a tree trunk and was pushed forcefully up against it.

"It's all your fault!"

I tried to speak, to defend myself, but couldn't get anything but gurgling sounds out of my throat. I gasped to breathe while he held me tight, pressing harder and harder till I thought I saw stars.

"They took my daughter because of you, you fool."

"Dad!"

The sound of his son's voice from the porch made the pastor let go of me, and I slid down onto the snow, coughing and gasping for air.

The pastor hovered above me, panting and wheezing in anger. He kicked me in the stomach, then bent over.

"Don't you ever show your face on my property again, you hear me? You and your little offspring better stay far away from my side of the property line, or I can't answer for what might happen to them."

I was still trying to catch my breath as he turned around and walked away. I saw him grab his wife by the arm and escort her inside, then slam the door behind him.

49

The door to her cell suddenly opened, and Savannah sat up. She had been sleeping, she realized and blinked her eyes in the darkness when someone appeared in the door.

"Come with me," the deputy said.

Savannah stood to her feet, feeling slightly confused. She passed a window in the sheriff's office and realized it was late. Surely, they hadn't woken her up to interrogate her again, had they? Would they be that cruel?

Savannah followed the deputy down the hallway, still yawning and trying to rub the sleep out of her eyes when she heard a scream. With a small gasp, she looked up. In through the door she was about to walk out of, came Penny. She was screaming and kicking like a mad person as two deputies almost carried her through the door.

When she passed Savannah, their eyes met, and Penny's were flaming in anger. The fire in them made Savannah pull to the side, pressing her back up against the wall.

"I hate you! I hate you!" she screamed, addressed at Savannah.

Scared at the hatred she saw in her eyes, Savannah felt her heart throb in her chest. Penny was taken away, screaming down the hallway, and Savannah looked after her. She felt the deputy's hand on her shoulder and turned to look up at him.

"Come."

Still in shock, Savannah walked through the double doors following the deputy and, much to her surprise, a well-known set of eyes waited for her on the other side.

"M-mom?"

Her mother smiled and held out her arms. Savannah looked at the deputy like she was asking for permission, and he nodded.

"She's here to take you home, Savannah. We know you didn't kill Benjamin, so you're free to go."

"I...I'm...what?" Savannah couldn't really figure out if they were messing with her or if it was true. She had thought she'd never get out again.

"You're free, baby," her mother said, tears rolling down her cheeks. "You can come home with me. Now."

Savannah looked at her mother, then finally threw herself in her arms and felt her warm breath close to her face. The smell of her hair was divine, and Savannah suddenly became very aware of how terrible she smelled herself after days of being locked up. Her mother sobbed, and her torso was throbbing. She kissed the top of Savannah's head and stroked her greasy hair gently.

"Come on, baby," she said and grabbed her hand in hers. Her eyes gleamed with happiness. "Let's go home."

With her mother's arm around her shoulder, Savannah was led out the back. The deputy said it was best this way and, as they stepped outside, she understood why. There was still a flock of local townspeople gathered in front of the entrance, holding signs in their hands with her name on them. They weren't yelling anymore like they had been when she was brought in, but they were still there, holding the signs up, telling the police they wanted *Justice for Benjamin* and that she should *get the chair* for what she did.

Savannah swallowed hard when seeing them in their thick winter coats, holding the signs up with their gloved hands, marching back and forth. Savannah's mom held the door for her, and she got into the car. Savannah looked out the back as they took off and wondered if the protestors would finally get off her back now that Penny had been arrested for the murder of Benjamin. Would she finally be able to live in peace or would this continue to haunt her for the rest of her days?

50

"Are you okay, Jack?"

Shannon opened the door for him. He looked terrible. He had that look to him like he was deeply shaken.

He sat down on a chair, breathing raggedly.

"What happened out there? Jack?"

He held a hand to his throat. It bore marks on it, and Shannon saw it now, while a sudden gush of fear ran through her.

"Jack?" she shrieked. "What are those marks?"

He swallowed and moved his head around as if to find out if his throat still worked.

"I'm fine. It was just...well, the pastor lost his temper with me and pushed me up against a tree. For a minute, I thought he would kill me. My throat is still hurting. Could you get me a glass of water, please?"

"Of course," she said and ran to the kitchen. She grabbed a glass and filled it, a sense of deep worry and fear rushing through her body. Jack drank greedily when she handed it to him.

"Should I call the sheriff?" she asked. "Do you want to report him for assault?"

He shook his head. "There's no need. As I said, I'm fine. I just need a minute to get back to myself. I think I need to lie down a little."

Jack got up, then walked to the couch and sat down, then leaned his head back. Shannon sat next to him. She kept staring at the red marks on his neck. A part of her remembered when her ex-husband had made similar marks on her throat once. She had tried to cover them up with make-up with no luck.

"So, what happened? Why did he get angry with you?"

"His daughter was arrested."

Shannon's eyes grew wide. "They arrested Penelope Rutherford?"

Shannon stared at Jack, quite surprised at the news.

"Yes. Her fingerprints were on the fire poker that they found earlier." He paused and looked around. "It's so quiet here. Did the kids go to bed?"

Shannon nodded and sipped a glass of water. "The movie ended, and they all turned in."

Jack looked at his watch. "I didn't even realize it was this late."

"I hadn't either. It was too late for Tyler. I should have put him down earlier. He got all whiny and wouldn't put on his PJs."

Jack chuckled. "So, what did you do?"

"I let him sleep in his underwear. If he keeps the covers on, he won't be cold. I couldn't get him to brush his teeth either. He kept screaming at me and running away. So, I gave up and just put him to bed. I didn't have the energy to fight with him. We can brush them extra in the morning."

"So, he's asleep now?" Jack asked.

"Yes, finally. It took forever. I hate how everything is a fight with him. I don't recall Angela being like that at that age."

"You probably just don't remember it. It's been a few years."

"Are you calling me old?" Shannon said with a glint in her eye.

He chuckled and pulled her close. They snuggled for a few minutes while Jack looked out the window.

"You're thinking about them, aren't you?" she asked. "You're thinking about the Rutherfords."

He nodded. "How can I not? Think about all they have been through. First, they lose their son and now...their daughter is taken in for having murdered him. That's gotta be tough."

Shannon put her head on Jack's chest. She could hear his heartbeat, and it made her feel comfortable. She understood why he wouldn't want to report the pastor after everything the man had been through over the past several weeks. Still, it made her furious with the man. Who did he think he was to attack her husband like that? She wanted to punch him for what he had done. He could have killed her beloved Jack.

"So, you think Penelope did it?" she asked. "Do you think she killed her own brother?"

He exhaled. "I don't know, to be honest. I feel like there's something we're missing here...like there is a lot more to this story than what we know. First of all, what makes a sister want to kill her brother? I think about Abigail and Austin. They can fight and be at each other's throats, but at the end of the day, they could never harm each other for real. Deep down, I know they love one another. How does a sixteen-year-old girl kill her own brother? And even if she did kill him, let's say in effect because of something going on between them, I could accept that. She got mad at him, then hit him with the fire poker, not really meaning to kill him, but only hurt him. But what about the others? Does that mean that she killed Lyle too? And Harry Mayer and followed Eliza Reuben in the truck? It seems like a lot for such a young girl to do. And it was all pretty cunning and well-planned, making them look like suicides. Does that fit the profile of a sixteen-year-old girl?"

Shannon shrugged, remembering her meeting with Benjamin's former girlfriend, Colette.

"Colette told me she seemed almost like she was in love with her own brother. She had even seen nude pictures of her on his phone that she believed she had sent to him. That was when she decided to break up with him. She couldn't stand it anymore. But Colette was terrified of Penelope and said she believed she attacked her in the parking lot behind the cinema. With what she told me, I'm actually not that surprised if she did kill those others as well. I've seen her up in that window of the house, and I keep feeling like she's looking down at us—like she's planning how to hurt us. That girl is not normal; I can tell you that much. Sending your brother nude pictures isn't normal. Not even close."

Jack nodded, but still seemed lost in his thoughts. "I just can't help but think that there is more to it than what we see. I want to be sure she killed Lyle. If only Austin would tell us what he saw."

Shannon sighed. "He will eventually. Give him time. You can't rush him into telling you."

"That's the problem," he said with a deep exhale. "I don't know if we have time. If they have the wrong killer, then who knows if or when there will be more?"

51

"Do you want seconds?"

Savannah felt her stomach and shook her head. "No, thanks. I am so full, Mom. It was really great, though."

She had made lasagna, which had been Savannah's favorite dish since she was just a toddler. Savannah had eaten like a horse, and now she felt like she was about to explode. She looked around in the trailer with a secret smile on her face. She couldn't believe she would ever be so happy to be back in this place. When they had first moved there, she had hated living in such a small space. Back in Newark, they had lived in a three-bedroom house with a yard, where she had a swing set and a big magnolia tree she loved to climb. Moving into this small trailer was hard on her, especially with the long winters where she could barely stand to be outside. The springs and summers were great, and she'd go biking in the mountains with Benjamin, but boy, the winters were tough. She hadn't learned to ski yet, so she was left out when her friends went up there on the weekends.

Her friends. The few she used to have. They were all gone now. As soon as Benjamin had disappeared, they turned their backs on her, thinking she somehow had something to do with it, that either she had hurt him so badly he had killed himself or she had killed him herself.

They were mostly his friends anyway. They had all known each other since third grade when Benjamin moved to the town. It wasn't easy making your way into a tight-knit group like that and finding a space. Now, she was probably never going to. Not without Benjamin. Even if she was cleared and the police no longer suspected her, it would still be this thing; it would still linger over her and in people's minds when they saw her. People never really forgot something like that, did they?

"Are you sure? There's plenty," her mother tried again. She fiddled nervously with the spatula.

"I'm good. Really, Mom. Maybe I can have the rest tomorrow for lunch. Now, I really just want to lie on my bed, a real bed, and enjoy being home. There's no place I would rather be than right here in this very moment. I can't tell you how happy I am to be home."

Her mother smiled. It wasn't a happy smile; it came off as concerned. "I think that's the first time since we moved down here that you've called this home."

"Well, that's what it is, and compared to where I've been, this is pure heaven."

Her mother looked at her fingers, then put the spatula down. Savannah noticed and gave her a look.

"Is there something wrong, Mom? You seem a little sad. Is there something you're not telling me?"

Her mother lifted her gaze, and their eyes met. The look in hers made Savannah wince.

"What's going on? You're scaring me, Mom. Please, tell me what's happening."

Her mother bit her lip, then took a deep breath.

"Mom?"

"I...I have to tell you something. It might be a little tough for you to hear. I wanted to wait till you had slept and felt comfortable again, but I'm not sure I can."

Savannah's heart dropped. What was going on here? She hadn't seen that look in her mother's eyes since they told her that her dad had cancer. Was something wrong with her mother? Was she sick too? Had she been to the doctor and received some bad news? Was Savannah going to be an orphan at the age of seventeen?

"Mom. You're scaring me now. What's going on?"

Her mother exhaled. "Okay. I guess I might as well tell you straight away. There is no other way around it. You need to know the truth, even though it will change the way you look at me forever."

52

Maggie Valley January 2019

"It's okay. You can come in."

Benjamin looked at Savannah, then pulled her hand. They were standing on the porch. Benjamin had picked her up, then taken her back to his house, much to her surprise. For the past many months, they had been sneaking around, ever since Benjamin's mother had that talk with him in the kitchen where she told him that they didn't want him to see her anymore.

"But...but what about your parents? They told you never to see me again," she said, surprised.

"They changed their minds," he said victoriously.

She wrinkled her forehead. "Why did they suddenly change their minds? They were pretty set on this. I heard your mother; I heard how she said there was no discussing it."

He pulled her into a kiss. A deep warmth spread throughout her body, and she felt her knees go soft. If she was perfectly honest, she wasn't too thrilled about the prospect of going back into his house again. She had enjoyed those past weeks when they had been going places, away from his family, away from his strange sister. This way she had Benjamin all to herself, even if it meant they had to pretend like they weren't dating in school and in front of friends. She had enjoyed keeping that little secret between them and just being them and no one else. Inside, behind that door, awaited Penny, and Savannah didn't really feel like having to face her again.

"I guess they just finally realize how nuts I am about you," he said with a wry smile. "Plus, I am seventeen; I'll be out of here soon. I guess they figured that they couldn't keep me from you."

She stared into his eyes, scrutinizing them deeply, then shook her head. "Yeah, I'm not buying that. There's something else. I can see it in your eyes, Benjamin. I know you. Tell me the truth, will you?"

He grinned, then sighed. "Okay. But are you sure you can handle the truth, though?"

Savannah bit her lip while wondering how bad it could be. Then she shrugged, deciding that if she didn't say yes, she'd wonder about this every time they were together, and that would be horrible. The cat was already out of the bag; she just didn't know what it looked like yet.

"Sure. I can handle anything."

He looked around, then pulled her toward the patio swing, and they sat down. Savannah felt her heart thump in her chest while wondering what he was going to tell her.

"Okay, so here's the deal," he said and took both her hands between his. "I don't mind telling you since it sort of involves you anyway. At first, I wanted to protect you against it, but I don't think that's very fair to you."

"Just tell me, will you?" she asked, feeling petrified.

He nodded, then took in a deep breath like he needed extra air for what he was about to say. "Here's the deal. The other week, I was looking for my dad. I had to ask him about some money for a pair of new sneakers that I really wanted; anyway, it doesn't matter, but I searched for him, and my mom said he was still at the church. So, I went there and walked into the back without knocking on the door.

In there, I saw them. He had his pants down and was on top of her; her skirt was pulled up. You can picture the rest."

Savannah stared at Benjamin, her eyes growing wider and wider. "Y-your dad was? With your mother?"

He laughed. "No, you fool. With another woman. He was having an affair with another woman."

"Oh. Wow. Really?"

"Yes, really."

"But...wait you said it had something to do with me. How does...?" She paused as the realization sunk in and her chest tightened. Suddenly, she could hardly breathe. "You mean...your dad and...?"

"And your mom, yes. They were at it like rabbits."

Her nostrils were flaring as she fought to keep her composure. "Your dad, the pastor, and...and my...*my* mom?"

He nodded. "Listen, I know it's shocking, and that's what I thought too. I was completely shaken at first, but then I realized, what the heck, might as well make something out of it."

"So, you told your dad that you wanted to be able to date me and in return, you wouldn't tell your mom about them?" she asked, puzzled at all this news, and a little baffled at her boyfriend's cunningness. It seemed kind of cold and devious.

"Bingo," he said. "But now that I told you, I've kind of broken that vow, so please promise me you won't tell. They can't find out."

Savannah didn't blink. She looked at her boyfriend. How was he not more devastated by this? How could he be so calculating as to use it for his own benefit? And just how was she supposed to keep it from her mother that she knew about her affair with the pastor? It changed everything for her. It even changed the way she felt about Benjamin. Suddenly, she felt this resentment begin to grow toward him and his family.

She hardly knew him at all, did she?

53

"We don't have enough eggs for tomorrow morning. I can't believe we've run out already."

Shannon came out of the kitchen and looked at me. I was still on the couch, while she wanted to clean up before we turned in. I was doing better, yet still shaken up by my meeting with the pastor in his yard. I couldn't stop thinking about those eyes that glared at me, the fire in them that I had seen. It wasn't quite the mercy and forgiveness I had expected from a man like him in his position. I didn't like the way the rest of his family looked at me and didn't even try to stop him, at least not at first. It had to be the oldest son who finally told him to stop. What was it about this entire family that gave me the creeps?

"What's that?" I asked, not sure I heard her right.

"We don't have enough eggs," she said and closed the door to the fridge. "I wanted to make scrambled eggs tomorrow morning for the kids, but we don't have enough."

"We could go for pancakes again," I said. "At Joey's Pancake House. I liked that place, and they had excellent pancakes. They were really good. The kids loved them too."

"I'm not really in the mood to go out," Shannon said. "I don't want to fight with Tyler or have to worry about the kids acting up. I need a quiet morning, please?"

"Didn't you just shop?" I asked. "I vividly remember carrying lots of bags in and putting eggs away."

"I did. I bought two packages of eggs just yesterday, but now they're gone. There's only one egg left, and that's hardly enough. I wanted to make this big breakfast with pancakes and scrambled eggs that we could eat together, all of us, as a family."

"I don't get it," I said, puzzled. "How did we use two packages of eggs in just one day?"

"There are a lot of kids in this house, Jack."

I could hear she was exhausted by the way she said my name and realized I had to save the day. I rose to my feet and grabbed the car keys.

"I'll go get some at the gas station. I think they're the only place open at this hour. Even the restaurants close at nine. But they ought to have eggs at the gas station, right? Don't try and answer that. I'll see for myself when I get there. And don't you worry. If they don't have them, I'll go someplace else. I won't stop till I find some."

She smiled, then approached me and threw her arms around my neck. "Would you do that for me? Would you really do that?"

I smiled back, tired but feeling good. I liked taking care of my family. "Of course, I will. Now, you go to bed, and I'll take care of the egg issue. I'll be right back."

I kissed her again, then sent her a comforting smile as she walked up the stairs. I grabbed my coat and put on my boots and readied myself to go back out into the freezing cold again. As I reached the Cadillac and got in, I looked at the house next door. I thought I saw the mother in the tower window again like I had on the first day we got there, but as I looked again, I couldn't see anyone there. I shivered, then cranked up the heat in the car before I took off.

54

Savannah stormed out of the trailer and left the door open behind her.

"Savannah? Come back here," her mother yelled from inside. "We need to talk about this."

But Savannah didn't stop. She didn't believe there was anything more to talk about. She wanted to get away as fast as humanly possible. She never wanted to see her mother again.

"Savannah!" her mother called from behind her in the darkness, but it was too late. Savannah was already on Soco Street, running as fast as she could, tears streaming across her cheeks.

How could you do this to me, Mom? How?

A car passed her from behind, rushing so fast past her that it slung snow into the air. The snow splashed onto her back, but Savannah barely noticed or even cared. All she could think about was what her mother had just told her and how to get as far away from her as possible.

"I hate this place," she mumbled into the night with a deep sniffle. "I really, really truly loathe this place. Everything went wrong from the second we got here."

I miss you so much, Dad. Why did you have to leave us like that? Why did you have to die? None of this would have ever happened if you were still around. Nothing has been good since you died. Nothing will ever be good again. I just know it won't.

Savannah stopped when she reached the old Ghost Town, or Ghost Town in The Sky, as it was officially named. She stared at the big sign out front and wondered about it. It used to be this amusement park but had closed down before Savannah moved to Maggie Valley. She had seen pictures of how it used to be, and many people in town still talked about it. Apparently, there was a chairlift that would take you up the mountain to an entire Wild West village with saloons with can-can dancers, a jail, and businesses along the main street that was the site of hourly gunfights. There had been roller-coaster rides and merry-go-rounds, trains running through town, and live country music playing in the Silver Dollar Saloon. It was built in the sixties, and it quickly became one of the largest attractions in the country, but after some visitors got stuck in the old rides, it had closed down some years ago. New owners had recently bought it intending to renovate and reopen it, but so far, it had been delayed because of some financial problems that the local paper wrote about a lot.

Savannah stood at the foot of the mountain by the building where you used to buy tickets to get up there and could see where the chairlift started when her phone vibrated in her pocket. It had been doing that ever since she stormed out of her mother's trailer, and she assumed it was her trying to get her to come back. She looked at the display and saw that she had called five times, but she didn't care. There was something else on her display, though, that caught her interest. It was a text from an unknown number. The words in it made her heart sink, and she read it over and over again, the phone shaking in her hand. Savannah dropped the phone into the snow, the screen cracking as it sunk through the wet snow and hit a small rock underneath. Savannah saw this through a curtain of tears, then turned her back on the phone that was still lit up in the darkness and walked past the sign and up the wooden stairs.

55

I had to drive almost to the neighboring town in order to find the eggs. The gas station was out, they said, and so I had to go a little further, outside of town, where I found a CVS that had eggs. It took an extra fifteen minutes, but I did so gladly. I knew it meant something to Shannon, and so I didn't mind. I had told Shannon to go to bed, so I assumed she was sound asleep.

I was listening to Lady Gaga singing with Bradley Cooper in my favorite song from their movie *A Star is Born* and cranked the volume up to its max and sang along. I had watched the movie with Shannon, and we had loved every second of it. The chemistry between those two was mesmerizing. I knew that Shannon believed they had to have a thing going in real life, but I believed they were just excellent actors. I didn't really care if they were an item or not; it was none of my business and shouldn't be anyone else's either, but it pleased me that Shannon wasn't touring at the moment. Part of me wished she would give it all up and just be with her family, but I knew that wasn't fair to her. She loved performing and writing music, and going away on tour was just a part of it. I just didn't like sharing her with the world.

As I drove back into town and down the main street, I slowed the car down. There were no other cars on the road, and everything was closed and left in complete darkness. Except for the chairlift behind the old Ghost Town in the Sky that I had heard so much about from locals, who were so proud of the place and still waited for it to reopen. The chairs were completely lit up all the way up the side of the mountain, and even more strangely, the lift was moving.

I drove past it, gaping at the lights all the way up the mountain. In the days we had been there, I hadn't seen that lift in motion or the lights turned on at all. Why would they turn it on at night? Were they testing the lift? As far as I knew, they hadn't even begun the renovation of the old Wild West town. Was someone going up there now? It was an odd hour to be turning on the lifts, I believed.

Thinking it was none of my business, I shook the thought for a few seconds and continued down the road. But even as I put it physically behind me, I still couldn't get it out of my system. Something was wrong here, and I didn't like it one bit. I pulled the wheel and turned the car around, then floored the accelerator and drove back into the parking lot in front of the Ghost Town in the Sky.

Heart throbbing in my chest, I killed the engine and got out. As my boot landed in the snow, I felt it kick something. I looked down to see what it was and spotted a phone in the snow. Puzzled at this, I picked it up and wiped the snow off, then pressed a button to make the display light up. The screen was cracked, but it still worked and had some battery left on it.

Whoever owned the phone had received a text from an unknown caller, but never opened it. I didn't know the password but could still read it without opening the phone. The words in the text made me understand whose the phone was and what was going on.

Feeling my pulse quickening, I glanced at the lift, pondering how far she had gotten. I put her phone in my pocket, then rushed up the stairs toward the lift, zipping up my coat on the way to keep out the cold. I put myself in position and let the next chair lift me into the cold air, worrying that I was too late.

56

I set my boots down on top of the mountain as the chairlift reached the end. It was completely dark up there, and it took a few minutes for my eyes to be able to see anything. I used my own phone to light up the path in front of me, and soon the beam landed on a snow-covered street with old western houses on both sides of it. It was completely dark, and all the houses were abandoned, making the title Ghost Town in the Sky more fitting than ever.

I walked down the street, lighting my phone on the wooden buildings with porches and swinging doors. There were about forty buildings that made me feel like I had just stepped inside of an old western movie. All I missed was the tumbleweed running down the main street and the gunfight, but instead, there was snow covering everything, making it even eerier.

"Savannah?" I called out. "Where are you?"

No answer came, and I continued walking, lighting up the buildings next to me, but not seeing any sign of life.

Come on, Savannah. Where are you?

I had never met the girl myself, but I had seen her picture in *The Mountaineer* several times where they wrote about the mystery of what happened to Benjamin Rutherford. The last time I saw it was after she had been arrested and the newspaper speculated that she might have kept him for days before finally killing him and putting him in the creek. How they could write that about a young girl and ruin her life without any evidence or police statement to back it up was beyond me. But I never understood the world of journalism much, and it was something I often debated with my friend Rebekka Franck.

"Savannah? Come on; speak to me. I'm not here to hurt you. I just want to talk to you for a few minutes. You don't know me, but my name is Jack Ryder, and I'm a detective. I don't think you killed Benjamin Rutherford. But I am scared of what you're planning to do to yourself right now. Please, don't do anything stupid, Savannah; please, talk to me instead."

The only answer I received was the howling wind. It hit me in the face and caused me to shiver. I really didn't want to be up there on the mountaintop in the freezing cold and darkness, staring at old abandoned wooden houses. I longed to be in my warm bed with my wonderful wife close to me.

"Savannah?"

I heard a sound coming from between two houses and gasped. I turned the light through the alley and spotted a viewing point behind it, with telescopes where you could probably see the spectacular mountain views in bright daylight. I also saw Savannah there, standing on top of a rock formation on the other side of the fence, balancing on the edge.

Oh, dear God, no!

I sprang forward and ran in between the houses, my heart racing in my chest "Savannah, no!"

She didn't notice me. The closer I got to her, the more I realized there was an abyss beneath her, and if she fell, she would definitely kill herself. She stood there like she was paralyzed and stared into the darkness.

"Please, Savannah," I said as I approached her. "Please, don't jump. Talk to me instead. Tell me what's going on."

She didn't even turn to look at me. She stood like a statue, balancing, her toes already over the edge. She had taken off her shoes and socks and placed them at the foot of the rock.

"Don't let them win," I said. "If you do this, they will. They'll think they were right about you; they'll always believe that you were guilty."

"And what if I am?" she asked.

"Excuse me?" I asked, puzzled. "You mean to say that you killed Benjamin?"

She paused a few seconds, then answered: "I might have. You don't know that."

"I don't know. You're right about that. But I do know that the police released you. I also know that you received a text a while ago where some mean person told you to kill yourself."

She turned her head and looked at me. I lit her up with my phone, then pulled out her phone.

"How do you know?" she asked, her voice hoarse, her breathing ragged.

I showed her the phone. "I found this in the parking lot. I didn't have to be a detective to figure out you turned on the lift to get up here."

She swallowed. "There was a small shed down there. I had to break through the glass to get to the button. It was locked, but I used a rock to break it. I flipped on the power, and then it was the easiest thing from there. My dad used to work part-time at an amusement park in the summer, and he would sometimes take me when I was a kid."

She turned to look into the darkness again. I wondered if I jumped for her now, if I could grab her or if me moving even an inch would only prompt her to take the plunge.

"Savannah, I know you think of it as an easy way out now, but this is not the solution. I'm sure that once the real killer is convicted, then no one will think you killed Benjamin. I'm sure it hasn't been easy for you these past few weeks when everyone has been thinking this about you, but they'll come around once they find out you didn't do it. You don't have to hurt yourself. You didn't do anything wrong. Give it a few weeks, and everything will go back to normal. You'll be back in school, and people will have forgotten."

"Is that what you think, Detective?" she asked. "That life will be able go back to normal for me?"

"I'm sure it will, Savannah. I know you're devastated over having lost Benjamin, and I heard that your dad died a few years ago, but please, Savannah. No one wants you to do this. Think about your mother."

"She's exactly the one I am thinking about," she hissed. "She's the reason I am even out here."

I lifted both eyebrows in surprise. "What do you mean? I thought she was happy to have you back?"

"She doesn't care about me," Savannah said, pushing herself an inch closer to the edge, so half of her feet were dangling over the edge. "She doesn't care about me at all."

"I think you're wrong about that," I said.

Savannah snorted. "She's pregnant; did you know that?"

I shook my head. "No, I didn't. But that only gives you another reason to stay here with us, with them, doesn't it? I mean you can't just leave now and never get to know your brother or sister, right?"

That made Savannah laugh out loud for some reason. The sound made me feel very uncomfortable. There was something in the tone of it that told me she had already made up her mind and there was nothing I could say or do to stop her.

"You think I ever want to meet the bastard that my mother is carrying? You think I ever want to have anything to do with my dead boyfriend's sibling? I mean...how sick is that?"

And just like that, the pieces fell into place, shocking as they were. "You mean to say that...your mom and...the pastor?"

She turned her head and looked into my eyes for just a second. I saw so much sadness in them; it almost broke me apart. As she stared at me, a smile grew from the side of her mouth, and the next thing I knew, she jumped.

57

The dark figure was getting into position, clutching the rifle between their hands, eyes scanning the area, looking for movement in the darkness. The snow crunched under their boots while birds took off from treetops as the figure found the perfect spot.

The cloud cover that had lingered most of the night above spread out and gave room for the moon to shine down on the glittering snow, making it a bright night. The moonlight made seeing easier and, as the figure spotted movement, the rifle was lifted up to the eye and placed in position. Through the scope, the figure spotted a red fox in the snow, then lowered the rifle with an exhale while the creature turned around and disappeared in between the trees.

The figure put the rifle down on a rock formation, leaning their elbow on the rock to steady it, then peeked into the scope. The figure saw the girl as she balanced on the edge of the rock.

"Come on, sweetie. You can do it."

The girl stood for a few minutes, looking down, while the figure watched her, ready to shoot should she change her mind. The body would then fall into the abyss and be buried in the snow where it wouldn't be found till the spring. By then, it would have been eaten by animals to the extent that there wouldn't be much of her left. And most importantly, the town would have found justice. They would say it was suicide after reading the text on her phone, and most people would believe she got what she deserved. But most importantly, the girl wouldn't be able to talk.

"Come on, jump. Just jump. Go for it."

The girl stayed in place, and that was when something happened that the figure hadn't counted on. Another person showed up, someone that the figure hadn't counted on as a threat.

The figure lowered the rifle and stared at them both when suddenly the girl jumped...and the man leaped after her.

58

I was faster than lightning. As soon as I realized what her intentions were, I leaped into the air and reached out my arm. I grabbed her literally in the air, and with my weight, I managed to push her to the side. We landed on a plateau below, my back hitting against the cliff, Savannah on top of me, me holding onto her so tight that she couldn't move. The air was knocked out of me, but we didn't stop there. We rolled to the side and soon we started to slide down, rocks and snow and dirt skidding down with us. I felt pain in my neck and leg, but held onto Savannah the best I could, sheltering her from being hurt. She screamed as we slid and soon came to a halt as we hit another ledge below, where we finally stopped completely in a pile of deep snow. Panting in pain, I rolled to the side and finally let go of Savannah. She cried.

"Are you hurt?" I asked.

"No," she said. "I scraped my knee and elbow, but that was it. How about you? Are you okay?"

I tried to sit up, but it hurt. I could barely move my back. "I am not sure. I think I might have hurt my back."

I blinked a few times and looked above us. We had to be about ten feet below the viewpoint. I had dropped both of our phones when I jumped for her. There was nothing but snow around us, snow and rocks.

"Oh, my God, I am so sorry," Savannah said, crying. "I can't believe I did this. It's all my fault. I am so so sorry. How will we ever get back up from down here?"

I tried to sit up, but it hurt terribly, and I had to lean back into the snow to ease the pain. I couldn't think straight. Savannah was about to panic. I closed my eyes and tried to think, but she made it hard.

"Calm down," I said.

Savannah sobbed. "I'm so sorry. I keep causing people so much pain. I should never have broken up with Benjamin. Do you know how often I have thought about that? If I hadn't done that on the porch that night, then maybe he wouldn't have died."

I swallowed, trying to press the pain and fear away, then reached out my hand and placed it on her back.

"Hey. You can't keep doing this to yourself. It wasn't your fault. He was killed. He suffered blunt force trauma to the back of his head, caused by a fire poker."

"A fire poker?" she said, surprised and concerned.

"The sheriff didn't tell you?" I asked.

"They just kept asking me the same questions over and over again and then suddenly they released me, and I saw Penny being brought in. Do they think she killed him?"

I exhaled. "I'm pretty sure they do."

"But...but she loves him," she said. "Why would she kill him? It makes no sense."

"You don't think she could have killed him?" I asked, surprised, almost forgetting I was in pain. "But...I don't understand. I thought you broke up with him because of her?"

"Their relationship has always been strange to me, yes. It's too much, too close for siblings, creepy even at times, and yes, that's why I broke up with him, but I can't...I can't imagine Penny ever hurting Benjamin. She loved him more than anyone on this planet."

"That does sound odd," I said and managed to sit up finally as the pain receded slightly in my back, making me convinced it could just be the blow and hopefully nothing important was broken. "But maybe she got angry with him because he didn't return her love for him? Because they could never be together? They did find her fingerprints on the murder weapon," I said. "It was a fire poker."

Savannah gasped.

"Her fingerprints were on the poker because she found it," she said. "Not because she killed him."

"What do you mean she found it?" I asked.

"She found the fire poker covered in blood inside the small shack on the property of their house. There was a hatch there, and she opened it and pulled it out."

"And how do you know this?"

Savannah sighed. "I've never told anyone this, but she came to me. The night before I was arrested, she came to me. She told me she knew what I had done and to admit to it now. She had found the bloody poker, and she had found her brother's body. I thought she was just going crazy."

I took a deep breath, trying to take in all this new information, wanting to ask the right questions while I had her opening up to me.

"She found the body? Before it showed up in the water?"

"For all I know, she might have placed him in the water," she said as the pieces fell in place in her mind. "That's what she told me she'd do if I didn't go to the police and admit to having hurt him with the fire poker and then hiding him in their freezer to make sure someone in her family was blamed. She thought I had tried to be clever and make sure the suspicion was not on me. She said if I didn't tell the sheriff what I had done, she'd release the body into the creek, and then when it showed up, I'd be arrested. I told her that I couldn't do that since I had nothing to do with it. I was certain she was bluffing —that it was just some insane story she had come up with, but the next day, he turned up in the creek just like she had told me he would."

"Did you tell this to the police?" I asked. "When they questioned you?"

"I told them to talk to Penelope, but they didn't want to listen. I figured they would never believe me. Why should they?"

It was a good question. One I didn't have an answer for, just like I lacked answers for so many other questions about this case. And just like I still hadn't figured out how the heck we were going to get away from this ledge before we both froze to death.

59

Shannon jolted upright in bed with a gasp. She felt her pillow and realized it was soaked. She turned to look in the bed next to her then realized that Jack wasn't there.

Could he still be out looking for eggs?

She found her phone on the nightstand and saw that it was two in the morning. Realizing that Jack should have been back a long time ago, she got out of bed and walked down the stairs, wondering if he had been afraid of waking her up and just decided to sleep on the couch. It seemed like something Jack would do. The needs of his loved ones always came before his own.

But he wasn't on the couch either.

"Jack?"

Shannon peeked out the window but couldn't see the car anywhere. Her heart dropped as she realized that Jack hadn't come back at all.

Fear rushing through her veins, she ran up the stairs and found her phone, then called him. As she feared, no one answered. She tried again, her pulse quickening.

"Come on, Jack, pick up. Come on!"

But still, there was no answer. She tried one more time, then hung up and grunted with agitation. She stared out into the darkness. He had been gone for more than two hours. Where could he be?

She wrote him a text, then stared at the phone while it sent when she remembered something. She had recently installed Mappen on all the phones in the family so she could keep track of all the kids.

Shannon opened the app and quickly found Jack's icon with a small picture of his face inside the bubble. She looked at the map and found his location, then shook her head. It didn't make any sense. Something had to be wrong.

Heart racing in her throat, she went outside and ran to the neighboring house, then knocked.

Mrs. Rutherford came to the door, a look of resentment on her face. "You? What do you want? Do you have any idea what time it is?"

"I know," she said, "and I am so so sorry. But my husband hasn't come back. He went to get some eggs and told me to go to sleep, and then...he's not come back and he's..." She lifted her phone to show the woman his location on the map.

"But that's...the old amusement park up on the mountain? It's closed. What is he doing up there?"

"That's what I don't know. But I have this feeling that something is awfully wrong. I need your help, please. I don't know where else to turn. I know you're not fond of any of us right now, but please, something might have happened to him."

Mrs. Rutherford exhaled. She shook her head. "I...I..."

"Please? From one mother to another?"

She sighed deeply. The two women locked eyes and reached some sort of understanding or maybe sympathy.

"Okay, then. How can I be of help?"

"I need a car to go look for him," Shannon said, her shoulders coming down slightly. "And then I need someone to keep an eye on my children while I go look for him."

Beatrice Rutherford nodded heavily. "All right. I can do that. I was up anyway. Hard to fall asleep when your daughter is in prison for something she didn't do." She reached inside and grabbed a set of keys, then handed them to Shannon. "You can take my son's truck over there. No one uses it anymore. Charles hasn't used it for years, not since the accident, so Benjamin took over driving it once he got his license, but he...well...as I said, no one uses it anymore."

Shannon swallowed hard when looking into the eyes of the grieving mother.

"Anyway," Beatrice Rutherford said, her voice heavy in grief, "I assume the door to your cabin is open. I'll go sit in the living room in case any of your children wake up."

"Thank you so much," Shannon said and started to walk toward the truck. "You have no idea how big a help this is. I'll be back as soon as I can."

60

Shannon parked the truck next to their Cadillac in the parking lot in front of the old amusement park. Shannon had heard about the place but didn't think it was open for visitors, especially not at this time of night. Yet the chairlift was lit up, and it was running.

Something's not right here.

Shannon didn't think about it any longer, she just slammed the car door shut, then rushed up to the lift. She sat in a chair and let it take her up in the air toward the unknown. She had no idea what waited for her up there, but she had a feeling it wasn't pretty.

Please be safe, Jack. Please be safe.

A huge knot in her throat, Shannon jumped off the chairlift and found herself in strange surroundings. Using a flashlight she had found in the truck, she lit her way through the old wooden Wild West buildings. As the flashlight hit the Silver Dollar Saloon, she gasped, thinking she saw someone standing up on the porch, but then realized it was probably just her imagination. She rushed ahead, following the two sets of footprints that she spotted in the snow, thinking one of them had to belong to Jack.

"Jack?" she called out, hoping he would hear her and peek out from somewhere. "Are you up here, Jack?"

The prints led her to a viewpoint with telescopes, and as she lit the area up with her flashlight, she spotted two cellphones lying on the ground by a big rock formation on the other side of the fence.

Shannon hunched under it, then hurried to them and picked one up that looked like Jack's and as she tapped in the code to open it, she realized it was his, then felt like she had to throw up. If his phone was there, then where was he? And whose was the other phone?

She reached over and grabbed it, then brushed snow off the cracked display and tapped the screen. Nothing happened, and she concluded it had run out of battery. But whose was it?

What is going on here, Jack?

Shannon sighed anxiously. She grabbed her own phone and was about to call the sheriff's office and report Jack missing when she thought she heard something, and it made her stop to listen. It sounded almost like two people talking, or were they moaning?

"Jack?"

Shannon stared into the darkness, then approached the huge rock and climbed up on it. Shannon had never been great with heights. She was an excellent skier and could rush down mountainsides, even in deep snow, but climbing a rock or going zip-lining always made her feel like she had to be sick. She never liked climbing walls or going up in tall towers.

"Jack?" she called again, louder this time. She couldn't escape this feeling that maybe...no, he couldn't be, could he? Could he have fallen over the edge somehow?

As she came closer to the edge, Shannon sat down on her knees and slowly pushed her self forward till she finally reached the edge and she knew nothing but darkness was beneath her. She closed her eyes and took in a deep breath, then peeked down below, shining her light into the abyss, then called at the top of her lungs, "JACK!"

61

Maggie Valley February 2019

Savannah was sitting at the table with the rest of Benjamin's family. The mood around the table was more than strange, and it made Savannah feel very uncomfortable. No one spoke unless it was to ask someone to pass something, and no one spoke to her or even looked at her at all. She sensed they didn't like her being there, even though Benjamin had told her it would be all right, that they had asked for her to come. She had a feeling he had just made that part up.

Midway through the dinner, consisting of chicken pot pie and cornbread, Mrs. Rutherford finally addressed her, forcing a smile, and looking into her eyes.

"So, Savannah, how's your mother doing? Is the campground doing well? I suspect there must have been a lot of renovations that needed to be done when you took over."

Savannah almost choked on her food, surprised that someone actually spoke to her.

"We're doing all right," she said. "We're fully booked for the summer, so it's actually going pretty well. My mom has been working really hard, so it's a pleasure to see her work pay off finally."

Penny dropped her fork demonstratively and rolled her eyes, while Charles Junior mumbled something under his breath that Savannah couldn't hear.

Savannah accidentally locked eyes with the pastor and was reminded of what Benjamin had told her about the affair. She felt her stomach churn at the thought and realized it had been a mistake to accept the dinner invitation. It was one thing to hang out with Benjamin and be at his house when it was mostly his sister who bothered them by staring at them or crawling onto the couch and snuggling with Benjamin, coming in between him and Savannah. But being at their dinner table, at least for the father, had to be a constant reminder of what he was doing to his family. She stared at her boyfriend, realizing Benjamin had taken it too far. They didn't have to rub it in his father's face like that. They could just date secretly, but that wasn't Benjamin's style. He seemed to enjoy this little show and couldn't stop grinning. Savannah didn't like to be used in their little games, whatever they were. She understood why Benjamin was angry with his father for what he was doing, but she didn't understand his need to torture him like this. It didn't seem to do anyone any good.

Mrs. Rutherford cleared her throat, then wiped her mouth on her napkin before addressing Benjamin.

"Can I see you in the kitchen, please?"

"Of course, Mother."

Benjamin's grin grew even wider like he had expected this, maybe even waited for it to happen. He rose to his feet and followed her into the kitchen, leaving Savannah alone with the rest of the family. The pastor wiped his mouth too and threw down his silverware. "I'm done," he said and emptied his glass, then rose to his feet and walked away.

"I'm done too," Penny said and glanced with disgust at Savannah before storming out of the room.

Charles Junior stayed in place for a few minutes, poking his fork into the chicken, pushing it around like he was just trying to be polite and keep Savannah company, so she wouldn't have to finish her food alone.

Savannah put her silverware down, then sent him a smile. "I think I'm done too."

Charles Junior nodded. He backed out from underneath the table in his wheelchair.

"Don't mind them," he said. "It's not your fault."

Charles smiled at her, then rolled away, while Savannah sat back wondering what the heck was going on with this family, and then wondered if she really wanted to be a part of it.

She rose to her feet and gathered the plates together, thinking she could at least help with the clean-up, and walked out toward the kitchen, pushing the door open with her hip. As she turned around, the plates still in her hands, she spotted Benjamin and his mother in the kitchen. Mrs. Rutherford was hovering above him, holding him down with her hand on his throat, her face red with anger, a knife lifted above him, held in a shaking hand, while she yelled, "Don't you dare say anything!"

Savannah dropped all the plates in surprise, and his mother looked up, then let go of Benjamin, who coughed and gasped for air. Heart in her throat, Savannah began gathering the remains of the shattered plates and cut her finger in the process, but Benjamin rushed to her, grabbed her by the hand, and pulled her away.

"What was that, Benjamin?" she asked as he pulled her forcefully toward the door. They went outside on the porch before he let go. Benjamin bent over to catch his breath. He had red marks on his throat from where his mother had held him.

"What happened? Benjamin? Please, talk to me."

He shook his head, then threw himself on the patio swing. "Just another day at the Rutherford household," he said.

"Just another day? What do you mean? She looked like...she looked like she was about to kill you, Benjamin!"

He sat up and put his hands behind his neck. "Relax. She'll never harm me. Not for real."

Savannah felt her heart rate go up as she wondered about this crazy family and what she had gotten herself involved in. Was Benjamin in trouble? Would they harm him if they got the chance?

Benjamin reached over and grabbed her hand in his, then pulled her into a warm kiss. Savannah realized she was freezing and shuddered as their lips parted.

"Are you in trouble?" she asked. "Should I be nervous about leaving you with them?"

"Don't worry about me," he said, grinning. She couldn't figure out if he was doing that to make her feel better or if it was some sort of defense mechanism in him, to smile when things got bad.

"I'll be fine. I promise you," he said. "Nothing will happen to me. They'll never dare to harm me."

62

I heard her screams through the daze. We had been down there for what felt like forever. I had lost track of time and couldn't really figure out if it was a dream or if it was real. Savannah was lying next to me, shivering in the cold. I had told her to get in as close as possible to me to make sure we kept each other warm, but little did it help. My pain had made me dizzy, and I felt like I was drifting—like I could no longer really figure out what was real and what wasn't.

But as I heard Shannon's screams cut through the night, I knew that I wasn't dreaming anymore. This was very real. I turned my head to look up. I couldn't see anything but noticed a flashlight as it rushed across the landscape, the beam hitting the trees in the distance, then next hitting close to where we were laying. We had been talking for a long time, Savannah and me, before she got so tired, she asked if it was okay that she dozed off. I guess I did so too, even though I had tried to stay awake. I was completely drained, and my body was aching all over.

"JAAAACK!"

I pulled myself up to a sitting position, my feet kicking some rocks that skidded down into the abyss.

"Shannon! Is that really you? Shannon?"

"Jack! Jack, are you down there?"

The beam of the flashlight was still searching but came closer now. I reached out a hand and managed to get it into the beam of light and waved. Savannah grunted in her sleep, and I held her gently while moving, so she didn't fall. We were still very close to the edge, even though I had pulled us closer to the back wall. There wasn't much space on the cliff for both of us.

"Shannon. It's me. I'm right down here!"

"Jack! Jack, I see you now," she said and moved the beam, so it landed on my face. "There you are, Jack."

I couldn't see her since she was in the darkness but never had I heard a sweeter sound than her voice. Lying there in the freezing cold, I had been terrified I'd never see her or the children again.

"Oh, Jack, how...how..."

I moved and woke up Savannah. She sat up, grumbling, still half asleep. "Someone's here," I said. "My wife found us."

"Really?" she asked, surprised.

I took her hand in mine and warmed it. "We're going to be fine, Savannah. I'm sure of it. I'll personally make sure you get to go home to your mother. I know you ran away from her. I know you were upset and angry at her, but you have to figure these things out. You're all she has right now, you hear me? She's the only mother you'll ever get, and suicide will never be a solution."

Savannah nodded. "I know. I'm sorry."

"Jack?" Shannon asked. "I am going to call the sheriff. He can help you up from there."

"Okay," I yelled back, and she disappeared for a few minutes. The wait felt longer than anything, which was odd, but now that I had gotten my hopes up of actually surviving this, my patience got smaller, and I just wanted to get back so badly.

"I found a rope," she yelled as she peeked over the edge again. "In one of the old houses. The sheriff is on their way, but I thought I'd lower my flashlight to you, so you can see."

"That is a great idea," I said and turned around to see better. Seconds later, I spotted something come toward us, dangling on the end of a rope. I grabbed the flashlight, then untied it and held it in my hand. I turned it on to better see where we were and how close we were to the edge. As the light turned on and I shone it on Savannah so she could look around her, a shot was fired from in between the trees on the other side of the valley.

63

"Savannah? Savannah? SAVANNAH?"

The girl wasn't moving. I knelt next to her, shining the light on her when another shot resounded through the crisp air. I shrieked and ducked down on top of her while turning off the flashlight. With that thing on, we were like sitting ducks.

"Savannah, are you okay? Savannah?" I said and turned her around. My hand felt something moist, and I knew right away that it wasn't snow. It felt sticky and thick between my fingers.

Oh, dear God, no! Please, don't let her be hurt.

"Can you hear me, Savannah?" I asked, leaning close to her mouth to listen if she was trying to speak. Her lips moved, but nothing but a gust of air came out from between them. Another shot was fired and, as I ducked, I heard Shannon scream above us, panic setting in.

"JACK!"

The shot echoed off the mountainsides and made it impossible to locate. I still tried to look in the direction I thought it was coming from, but I couldn't see anything in the darkness. The trees on the other side were dense and looked like dark shadows.

"Get down, Shannon," I yelled up at her. "Lay down or get cover somewhere. You risk getting hit."

"Are you okay, Jack?" she said, her voice quivering.

"I am, but Savannah is hurt. We need to get her out of here, fast. How long before the sheriff arrives?"

"I...I don't know. They were on their way, but the sheriff was still in bed. He said he'd come as fast as possible."

Another shot resonated and Shannon screamed again. My entire body trembled as I ducked down and covered Savannah. My cheek was smeared in her blood.

"We need to get out of here," I yelled up at her. "We can't stay down here any longer, or we'll all die."

"But...but how?" Shannon asked.

"Lower the rope, and I'll try and see if I can get it around her and you can pull her up," I said.

"But they'll shoot at her and at us."

"We have to take that chance," I said. "We can't stay here. She's lost a lot of blood already. Her shirt is soaked. She doesn't have that long."

"Okay," Shannon said. "I'll try."

I exhaled, feeling hopeless. Shannon was strong, but I wasn't sure she'd be strong enough to pull Savannah up the side of a mountain. I still felt like we at least had to try.

Another shot blasted through the air, and I screamed and threw myself face flat in the snow. As I dropped down, my foot slid out over the edge, and soon I was skidding sideways toward the edge, grabbing for something to hold onto, but only finding snow and small rocks. I screamed as I slid toward the edge of the ledge, my fingers digging deep, desperate to find something, anything to grab, but not finding anything. Soon, I slid over the ledge and dropped into the abyss below.

64

"JAACK!"

The last thing she had heard from him was his scream. Shannon felt anxiety as it rushed through her body. Jack wasn't answering her anymore. What happened to him? Had he been shot?

Shannon was sitting behind the rock formation, hoping it would provide enough of a cover for her not to be hit by any of the projectiles. She felt like screaming but knew she had to keep her cool.

"Jack?" she said again. "Are you there, Jack?"

She closed her eyes in fear when there was no response. She took a few deep breaths, wondering what to do next. Something had happened to Jack, but she couldn't stand up and look over the cliff since she risked being shot. She couldn't just sit here either.

She heard a noise and opened her eyes just in time to see the sheriff and his deputies jump off the chairlift and rush toward her. Behind them followed a crew of mountain rescuers in their red suits, carrying a stretcher with them. The sight made Shannon almost burst into tears.

"What's going on?" Sheriff Franklin said, ducking down as he ran to her, a hand on his weapon. "We heard shots being fired."

"There's a shooter," Shannon said, breaking down and crying helplessly. "Someone's shooting at them down on the ledge. The girl was hit; Savannah is hit, and Jack isn't answering anymore."

The sheriff and his deputies pulled their guns and took cover.

"We need to get to them," Shannon said. "They're hurt. They need our help; please, help them."

Sheriff Franklin and Deputy Winston shared a look, and the sheriff nodded. Deputy Winston got up on his knees, then sliding himself forward, he reached the edge and peeked down, lying on his stomach. He shone a flashlight down there briefly, then returned.

"I see the girl. She's on a ledge further down, about ten feet. She's lying completely still, doesn't seem to be conscious, didn't react when the beam of light hit her."

"Is she alive?" the sheriff asked.

Winston shrugged. "Hard to tell."

"What about Jack?" Shannon asked, panicking. "Did you see Jack?"

Winston shook his head. "I'm sorry."

"But he was down there," Shannon said. "Just before. I spoke to him. He's there somewhere. He's got to be."

Sheriff Franklin looked troubled. "We need to get to the girl first; then we can look for Detective Ryder afterward."

Shannon knew they were right, but it still felt devastating to her. She took a deep breath and watched as the men in red suits found their gear and started lowering one of the rescuers into the darkness while the deputies kept in position, ready to reply if another shot should be fired.

Minutes that felt like hours went by while Shannon worried anxiously about Jack.

"I got her," the rescuer yelled as soon as he got Savannah strapped into the stretcher. Four men started to pull, and soon Savannah was placed on the ground next to Shannon. As she looked at her and the paramedics' lights fell on her, Shannon gasped when she saw the amount of blood. Jack had been right. She had lost a lot of blood. The rescuers examined her, and then Shannon heard the sound of an approaching chopper that soon stopped above their heads. Shannon watched as Savannah was airlifted into the chopper and taken away, her heart bleeding for the girl, but also for Jack. Two of the rescuers went with her and only left two others behind. The rescuer they had lowered down there was still looking for him but hadn't found him yet.

"I'm gonna try and go lower yet," he said over the radio to the others.

As the minutes passed, Shannon listened to her own heartbeat grow quicker, while preparing herself for the worst. Would she make it as a single mom? Would she be able to handle six kids on her own? Would she be able to live without Jack at all? Did she want to?

The thoughts made her start to cry, and she pushed them away. There was another scratch on the radio, and the voice sounded again.

"I can't see anyone."

"Got it," the sheriff replied. He looked at Shannon. "And you're absolutely sure he's down there, right?"

"Yes! Of course, he's down there. I spoke with him just before, and then there was a shot, and then he...he screamed, and then he didn't say anything anymore. But I am telling you he's down there."

"He could have fallen into the denser part of the forest further down," the man said on the radio. "I have no way of getting in there."

Sheriff Franklin exhaled and shook his head. "I'm sorry, Shannon. We...there's only a few hours to daybreak. Then it'll be easier to see him. We need more men to search the area down there. It's impassable; I'm afraid."

Shannon stared at him, mouth gaping. "So...what exactly are you saying? Are you telling me you're giving up; is that it?"

Sheriff Franklin held out a hand. "Not giving up, but we have to wait till I can get more men here."

"But...but why aren't they here already? And why can't they just go down there?" she said and pointed at the men standing by the edge, ready to help the rescuer get back up.

"We need men who are trained for this," the sheriff said. "I've called it in, and there's a patrol coming from Ashville, but it'll take about an hour or so. I'm sorry."

"An hour? He might be hurt! He might be bleeding to death down there, and you're telling me we have to wait an hour before we can even look for him? I can't believe this."

"As I said, I'm sorry, ma'am. We're doing everything we can to help find your husband."

Shannon stood to her feet, nostrils flaring. She stared into the darkness in front of her, then turned around and left.

65

"Wait for an hour. It'll be over my dead body," Shannon mumbled as she walked back to the western town. She kicked the snow angrily, then walked to a small cabin that had nothing to do with the rest of the amusement park. The door was easier to open this time than it had been earlier when she came looking for rope. She stared at the old pair of skis and the stretcher leaned up against the wall. The equipment had to be from the sixties, so it was old and outdated, but when she had seen it earlier, she had known this could be her last resort if it came to that.

She pulled everything out, then closed the door where the old weathered sign said SKI PATROL.

The wooden skis were very long and were going to be hard to maneuver, but luckily, Shannon had been a skier all her life, even back when the skis were longer and more difficult to maneuver. She even knew how to tie them to the old type of boots they wore back then. She put on the white uniform and then strapped the soft boots on.

The stretcher was worn out and could probably barely hold anyone, but she had to try. She exhaled deeply to remove the nervous feeling, then dragged the stretcher after her to the edge, choosing a place where the snow seemed thick and safe enough. Shannon paused as she looked down into the darkness, then glanced one last time toward the sheriff and his men. Sheriff Franklin was talking to his deputies when he saw her.

"Mrs. King? What are you doing?" he said and took a step toward her. "Hey, what do you think you're doing?"

"Sorry. I have to find him," Shannon said, took in a deep breath, and let her skis drop over the edge.

"Mrs. King!" the sheriff yelled behind her. "STOP HER!"

But it was too late. Shannon was skidding down the icy side of the mountain, the skis sliding, unable to find a grip. Then she made a jump and landed in the thick snow, the stretcher following behind her. Now, Shannon had been skiing in powder snow her entire life, so she knew how to maneuver through it, even though she could barely see anything in the darkness. She took it one turn at a time, keeping her weight equal on both skis, making her turns round, keeping the speed high since if she went too slow, she'd not be able to float to the surface between the turns. Shannon knew the more aggressive she was, the better, and made sure she was keeping the rhythm, so she took the energy from one turn to the next, bouncing off the snow. She kept her composure tight, not knowing what might be underneath and ready to take that unexpected bump when it occurred, keeping her feet moving, flexing her legs like she was skiing moguls, sinking in and bouncing off the white powder, sometimes hitting icy parts and sliding sideways, at others getting stuck in the deep snow, finding it hard to ski out of it. But soon, she was past the ledge that Jack and Savannah had been on and narrowing in on the dense forest below.

"Jack?" she called. "Are you here? JACK?"

Shannon skied in between the trees, trying to slow down a little to make sure she didn't slam into a tree trunk as it grew denser still. She skied between them, taking short turns, zigzagging between the trees, looking ahead and constantly preparing for the next turn, remembering she had a stretcher that needed to come with her, making the turns just big and round enough for it to follow, yet keeping an aggressive stance.

"Jack?" she called out again as she rushed in and out between the trunks, missing one by an inch, and slamming the stretcher into it, making it fly.

"Shoot," she said and stopped. The stretcher had been detached from her but seemed otherwise fine. She walked sideways up toward it and managed to grab it and reattach it to her when she heard someone moan.

"Sh...Shannon?"

66

"Jack? Is that you? Where are you?"

I could see a figure in the snow not far from me but wasn't sure if it was just a shadow. Not until it spoke. I had been woken up by cries that I was certain sounded like Shannon's voice.

"Shannon? Is that you?" I said, trying to move, but felt a sharp pain in my knee and remembered hitting it on a rock while sliding down the side of the mountain.

"Jack. Yes, it's me. Where are you, Jack? I can't see you."

"I see you. I'm behind you," I said as I reached forward, wincing in pain, then grabbed a small tree halfway covered in snow next to me and began to shake it violently. The leaves rustled and lumps of snow fell from it, but it made just enough movement for Shannon to see it.

"Over here!" I yelled.

The moving tree caught her eye, and soon she waved with her pole, almost screaming as she spoke.

"Now I see you, Jack. Stay where you are. Don't move a muscle. I am coming to you."

I let go of the branch, then leaned back in the thick snow, feeling the soreness in my entire body. Shannon approached me on her skis, then stopped and bent down to me.

"Oh, dear God, Jack. I was afraid I had lost you," she said, breathing raggedly from the heavy skiing. "Are you all right?" she asked, almost in tears. "Are you hurt?"

I nodded. "My knee and my back. I tried to get up but couldn't. I hurt my head too somehow when falling and passed out. I'm not...I'm still feeling dizzy."

"I need to get you down from this mountain and to a hospital as fast as possible," she said. "I brought a stretcher. I need to get you into it, and then I'll take you down."

"You can do that?" I asked, surprised.

"I actually worked as ski patrol back in college. I know how to do this."

I couldn't see her eyes properly but looked into them anyway, gratefulness overwhelming me.

"I think if you help me by lifting me up, then I can drag myself to the stretcher."

Shannon nodded. She unstrapped her skis, then sunk into the deep snow as she walked to my backside and reached down and pulled me up. It was hard for her because of the thick snow, but she managed to lift me just enough for me to grab the edge of the stretcher and roll myself onto it. Then she strapped me in till I couldn't move anymore and kissed me.

"You ready for this? I don't know the terrain, so I don't know what waits for us on the way down."

"You're amazing. Do I say that to you enough?"

Shannon chuckled and strapped her skis back on.

"I'll expect to hear it more from now on. Now, hold on tight, you're in for a bumpy ride."

PART IV

67

It was probably the worst hangover of his entire life. When Douglas Rutherford woke up on the bank of the creek, he hardly knew where he was or how he had gotten there. It took him a few minutes of going back to the night before until he finally remembered.

Now, three days had passed, and he had been hiding in an empty cabin where he had looked for shelter after waking up, soaked and freezing. It had a small fireplace that he used, and the people who had been there last had been kind enough to leave a couple of cans of food that he lived on. The closet had clothes that he could change into. There was also a first aid kit that he had used to bandage his shin. He had lucked out, and it didn't seem like it needed stitches after all.

And best of all, he hadn't had a drink in those three days, making his thinking clearer and his judgment a lot better. He didn't dare to leave the cabin, fearing the killer might see him and try to finish him off once again, so he had decided to wait a few days until things calmed down and no one would be looking for him anymore.

Did the killer think he was dead? That's what he hoped. If he stayed hidden long enough, the killer would have to reach that conclusion at some point, right? Or maybe there would need to be a body before his attempted killer would give up.

Douglas sighed deeply and went down on his knees to put more wood in the fireplace, wondering how long he would be able to hide in this place and where he would go when he ran out of food.

There's only one way this gets solved, and you know it. You can't run from the truth anymore. You have to tell.

68

"**K**nock, knock. Anyone home?"

I exhaled, relieved when Shannon peeked inside my hospital room. Her smile lit up all the grayness and dull light.

"Boy, am I glad to see you."

I sat up straight as she entered, my back still in pain. I grunted, annoyed at feeling like an old man who couldn't even move around properly in bed.

"Has the doctor been through on his rounds yet?" she asked while changing the flowers in my vase. I had been three days at the Haywood Regional Medical Center, and Shannon had made sure I had fresh flowers in my room every day. She and the kids had been here with me every day for hours to make it less unbearable to have to spend my vacation in the hospital. They said I had hurt my back, but nothing was broken. Apparently, there was a swelling in my head that they needed to monitor. It caused me to feel drowsy, but luckily, I felt no disorientation.

"Yup," I said.

"And?"

"And...he had good news. He got the test results back last night from the latest scan, and the swelling is down. I'm being discharged this afternoon." I grabbed Shannon around the waist and pulled her close. She shrieked happily, and I held her in my arms and kissed her.

Shannon sighed and stroked my cheek.

"You saved my life the other day; you do realize that, right?" I asked.

"Just like you have saved me again and again from my addictions," she said. "It's what we do. You and me."

"I still can't believe what you did. You could have been killed with that shooter after us."

"Is the sheriff any closer to finding who it was?" she asked.

I shook my head. The sheriff and his deputies had been my guests almost as much as my family had been the past three days. I had told them everything I knew about Eliza Reuben, Lyle Bishop, and Harry Mayer, and they were taking this very seriously, combing the entire area, doing their best to track down who this person was that had shot at me and Savannah Kelsey out on that ledge. So far, their investigation had only led to dead ends. But one thing was certain, whoever it was wanted us dead. If he was only gunning for Savannah or if I was on his list as well, we didn't know. But I had a feeling that even if I might not have been on the list before, I most certainly was now.

"They're still working on it, though," I said, trying to sound like I was convinced they would find this person. I didn't want Shannon to worry that any of our lives were in danger. We had to stay for at least a few more days because even though I'd be discharged this afternoon, I had to come in for new tests and at least one more scan, the doctor had told me. Besides, I was in no condition to drive for nine hours in a car anyway. I was so tired all the time and still had throbbing headaches. And my back was still recovering from the blow it had suffered, which meant it needed rest and being able to lie down.

"I'm sure they'll find him. Right now, they're tracing that text that someone sent Savannah, telling her to kill herself. They think it might have been the shooter, who probably followed her and wanted to make sure that she actually killed herself, or else he would make sure she died by shooting her. Whoever it was wanted to make sure Savannah was dead."

Shannon shook her head as her eyes grew wet. "It's so unfair. Why did she have to die? She was just a young girl."

I sighed deeply. It was the same question I kept asking myself while spending hours in this terrible bed, unable to sleep properly because of my back. Savannah had been shot on that night and had still been alive when she was taken away. She died of a cardiac arrest in the helicopter when they had almost reached the hospital. It was unbearable to think about, and it made me so angry, yet I couldn't stop myself from thinking about it. I was certain that this shooter was the same person who had killed Lyle and Harry and tried to kill Eliza. He was getting rid of these people for a reason, and I desperately wanted to find out what that reason was. I had been with Savannah on that ledge and failed to save her. The least I could do was to get justice for her and put her killer behind bars. I owed her that much.

So far, the sheriff still believed Penny had killed Benjamin, and they were building their case, but I wasn't so sure they were right. Not after Savannah told me that Penny had come to her and told her she had found the fire poker and her brother's dead body and that she didn't know what to do, that she wanted Savannah to turn herself in. That was why her fingerprints were on the murder weapon. I had told the sheriff all this, but he wasn't convinced. He believed Penny only did that to push the suspicion away from herself.

"How are the kids?" I asked, missing them. "You didn't bring them here today?"

She shook her head. "Bridget said she'd look after them while I came to see you. They were playing in the snow in the yard when I left. They were having a lot of fun, and it was the first time I had heard them laugh in days, so I figured I'd just let them stay."

"Gosh, I wish I could be with them," I said, thinking about the other day when I had been out there alone with them, having the time of my life. That was how I had wanted to spend my vacation, that and on the mountain whooshing down the slopes. Not in a gray hospital bed surrounded by strangers most of my day. I was sick of being here.

"How's Austin?" I asked. "He hasn't talked much to me the times you've brought him here."

She shook her head again. "I don't...I don't think he's doing so well, Jack. I can't get him to do anything with the rest of us. He's barely eating or sleeping. All he does is sit in that living room drawing while all the others have fun or like today when they're goofing around outside and building snowmen and having snowball fights. By the way, we found an old metal flyer sled in the back that they're pulling each other on across the yard; it's loads of fun. I asked Austin to come with us and to get some fresh air, but he doesn't seem to want to go outside at all."

I nodded. "He might feel guilty about me being hurt, thinking it was his fault. I'll talk to him when I get back today. Hopefully, he'll feel better once I'm with him again."

69

Maggie Valley 2019
January 25th
11:35 P.M.

SAVANNAH DROVE into the driveway with a deep exhale. She looked at her phone, then sent Benjamin a text.

I AM HERE. COME OUT ON THE PORCH. I DON'T WANT TO GO INSIDE, PLEASE.

She saw movement in the window, and soon the door swung open. Benjamin stepped out on the porch. Savannah watched him for a second, smiling secretively. She loved him so dearly, she really did, but she had decided she couldn't take anymore. She didn't know what was going on in his family, but whatever it was, she knew she didn't want to be a part of it. Especially not now with their parents being involved with each other. It was a mess and seemed like it could blow up at any second. Savannah didn't want to have to choose sides when it did. She was angry at her mom for what she had done, yes, but she was her mother and the only family she had left. She wasn't sure she loved Benjamin enough to pick him over her own mother. This was the right time to get out. Between his strange sister and his mother attacking him in the kitchen, she had realized that things were getting a little too tense and complicated for her taste. Next year, she'd go off to college, hopefully, if she landed that scholarship she had applied for, and then she'd be out of there. They could all keep their secrets and troubles to themselves. She was going out in the world to make a life for herself.

Savannah opened the door, and it creaked. Benjamin was walking back and forth, pacing as she approached him. He leaned over to kiss her, but she pulled away.

"What's going on here?" he asked anxiously. "Why are you pulling away and why are you asking to meet me out here?"

She cleared her throat. She had rehearsed her speech on the way there, but as she opened her mouth to speak, the words didn't come as she had wanted them to. They got stuck in her throat and came out all backward when they finally left her lips.

"I need space. I...all this with my mom and your...dad."

"Sh, don't talk so loud," he said. "My sister is right in there, and she doesn't know anything."

"I'm sorry," she said and handed him the necklace that he had given her back when she had forgiven him for buying the same one for his sister. "I can't do this...not anymore."

"So, what...?" he asked looking at the necklace in his hand. "You're breaking up with me?"

She nodded, biting her lip. "I am."

"But...why? And don't say it's my sister again. I'm sick of hearing that song."

Savannah shrugged. "It *is* because of her and...well, everything else. Your mom attacking you, our parents. It's just too much, Benjamin."

He grabbed her hand and held it tight in his, a little too tight. He was hurting her.

"You don't get to give up on us; do you hear me? I love you. We love each other. We are so good together, remember? You can't leave me. Not now. I need you Savannah, please."

Seeing him beg her like that somehow made her desire to get away from him even stronger. She looked into his eyes, then tilted her head, realizing something was off. He was sweating, even though it was freezing out. "What's going on, Benjamin?"

"How about we elope, huh? We can run away tonight. I'll go up and pack now, and you can pack your stuff, and we'll go wherever the old truck takes us, drive till it can't drive anymore. What do you say? Please, say yes, Savannah, please?"

"I...I can't, Benjamin. I have my mother here. It'll kill her."

"Please. I can't stay here. I need to get away."

"Why? Why Benjamin?"

He looked at the window nervously, and Savannah wondered about what she had seen in the house the last time she'd been there for dinner. Was he afraid of his mother?

"What's going on, Benjamin? Tell me!"

He reached into his pocket and fiddled with something, then took her hand and put it inside of it. He closed her hand.

"Here. Keep this somewhere safe. If anything happens to me, promise me you'll make sure the police and reporters get this, okay?"

She gave him a strange look. "I don't understand; are you afraid something might happen to you?"

"Just say you'll do it, okay?"

"O-Okay."

"Don't look at it," he said. "Just go. Hide it somewhere safe."

Savannah swallowed, then walked slowly to the car, glancing back at him a few times anxiously.

"Go," he said, urging her along. "Leave."

70

Shannon picked me up at the hospital at three o'clock. I had all my things, including her latest flower arrangement gathered, and was sitting on my bed when she entered pushing a wheelchair.

"Your chariot has arrived," she said, smiling.

"Very funny," I said. I walked to the chair, then slid into it. Shannon placed my bags in my lap and rolled me out of the room. I couldn't wait to see something other than gray walls and white coats. Nurse Sawyer stood in the hallway and grabbed my hand as I rolled past her.

"Come and say hi to us when you get the chance," she said. "You'll be missed."

"Not sure I'm gonna do that," I said, chuckling. "I'm kind of tired of hospitals."

"Fair enough," she said, laughing. "But it was nice to meet you and your lovely family. Say hello to the children for me, especially Tyler. He's a hoot."

"Will do," I said. "And, yes, he is."

We continued further, and I asked Shannon to let me pay Eliza

Reuben a short visit before we took the elevator down. Her door was open, so I rolled right in after saying hello to the deputy guarding outside. Eliza was still keeping herself barely alive with machines, and there had been no new development in her condition, the sheriff had told me. I wanted to see for myself, though, and now I was staring at her, her chest heaving, her eyes moving behind the lids, but other than that, she seemed more dead than alive.

I asked Shannon to roll me close to her and grabbed Eliza's hand in mine. A tear escaped the corner of my eye as I whispered in her ear.

"I will find whoever did this to you and to all the others and I will make sure they never see daylight again. You mark my words. This is my promise to you."

I squeezed her hand in mine and let the tear roll down my cheek before signaling to Shannon that I was ready to leave. Shannon grabbed the handles of my chair and rolled me out. At the hospital entrance, we stopped, and Shannon helped me get up and out of the chair. Holding onto her, I took a few steps, and the doors slid open so I could feel the cold, fresh winter air. I took a deep breath, still holding onto Shannon, and she handed me a cane.

"I bought it."

"Why? I don't want a cane."

"Yes, you do, Jack. You need it. It's just till your back is better."

I stared at the cane in my hand. "I'm gonna look like an old man," I said. "Even more than I feel."

Shannon gave me a look that told me this was not up for debate. "Don't be vain now. As long as your back and your knee hurt, you're gonna need something to lean on. There's no shame in using a cane."

"All right," I said when realizing this was one area she wasn't going to budge on. As I took a few steps leaning on the cane, I realized it wasn't too bad.

Shannon held the door to the Cadillac for me, and I got in, placing the cane between my legs. As we drove out of the parking lot,

I rolled my window down and stuck my head out like a dog, taking in all the wonderful fresh air that didn't smell like hospital.

As we reached Maggie Valley and drove up the main street, I placed a hand on Shannon's shoulder.

"There's something I need to do first before we go to the cabin."

"Okay?" she asked. "What is it?"

"Take a turn here. There's someone I need to talk to."

71

Savannah's mom looked like she had lost ten pounds in the past few days. She stood in the door to her trailer. Shannon stayed behind Jack, wondering what he was up to now.

"I think you know who I am," Jack said as the woman's eyes fell on him.

"Detective Ryder," Susan Kelsey said, nodding with surprise. "What are you doing here?"

"Paying my respects. I am so sorry for your loss, and I am so angry at myself for not being able to save your daughter."

Susan exhaled. "Maybe you'd like to come in?"

"Yes, please. Thank you," Jack said and walked inside, using his cane to help him up the stairs.

"Can I get you something to drink? Water? Coffee? A soda?" she asked, her voice quivering.

"Coffee sounds absolutely wonderful," Jack said. "What I got at the hospital was barely drinkable."

"Let me make it for you while you two talk," Shannon said and walked to the kitchen while Jack sat down at the small table in the trailer.

"Thank you," Susan said, with a heavy sigh.

Shannon found the coffee maker and some beans, then put on a pot. The machine soon sputtered and spat out thick black coffee that she poured into three cups and served. Then she sat down. Jack had been telling Susan about the last minutes with Savannah on the ledge, getting into the details of how she fought for her life.

"She told me many things while we were out there," Jack said, "while we waited for help and thought we would end up freezing to death. She told me that Penny had come to her and said she had found Benjamin's body. But there was also something else she told me that I haven't been able to forget."

Susan sipped her coffee and Shannon did the same. It was a little strong, but it would have to do. Jack seemed to enjoy it and made happy sounds as he took his first sip.

"And what is that?" Susan asked.

"She told me that Benjamin gave her something on the night he disappeared. She went to him to break up with him, but then he handed her something that he told her to take good care of and make sure was given to the police or a reporter if anything happened to him."

Susan looked surprised. "Really? And just what was that thing?"

"A flash drive," Jack said and sipped his coffee again. "A flash drive containing information that no one wanted to get out."

"Really? I never heard of that."

"I have a feeling you have since Savannah also told me that you and she looked at it together. Once she got back, you were sitting in the kitchen, and she told you about what he had said and given her. You plugged it into the computer and looked at it. And what did you see?"

"I have to say...I don't know what you're..."

"Allow me to help your memory then. You saw a series of articles written by a journalist called Eliza Reuben. The articles were about a crash in 2010 in Oklahoma. The circumstances surrounding the crash were more than suspicious since there were two cars involved but only one driver was still there when the police and paramedics arrived, and he was dead. So was his wife. The driver of the other car had mysteriously vanished and was never found. What was even stranger was that the couple who had died in the car crash had a son, an eight-year-old boy, and he was nowhere to be seen. He was never found."

"Okay, so I might have read some articles about that, yes," she said with a shrug. "But I didn't even know what they were about or why they were important."

"But they weren't the only thing you saw on that flash drive; there was something else," Jack said, sipping more coffee. Shannon sensed the tension grow in the trailer and felt uncomfortable. Jack looked into Susan's eyes.

"There was also a letter. A letter written by eight-year-old Benjamin, recalling in detail what he saw the day his parents died in a car crash."

———————

72

"I had a lot of extra time while in the hospital, and so I started to look into what Savannah had told me. It didn't take me long to find out that the woman who was killed in that crash was your sister, Maria, which makes Benjamin your nephew and Savannah's cousin. It also fits with the dates for when the Rutherfords came to town with their—now—three children, moving here from Oklahoma. I spoke to a nurse—a very nice woman—who was a local to Maggie Valley. She told me they bought the house next to where we're staying in 2010, only a few weeks after the accident that had crippled their oldest son, Charles Junior."

Susan shook her head. "I don't know anything about all that; I..."

"Charles Junior killed your sister and her husband, didn't he? Right after the crash, he called his parents and told them what had happened and that he couldn't walk. He also told them he was driving while drunk and they knew he would end up in jail for killing those two people if the police were involved. So, instead of calling for help, Mrs. Rutherford and the pastor drove out there to help him themselves. They carried Charles Junior into their car and, when realizing Benjamin was still alive, they took him with them too. He wrote all this in his letter from back then, in detail of how he was trapped inside the car when they arrived, and the pastor helped him get out. Next thing, they packed everything they owned and moved down here, where the pastor found a position in the middle of nowhere, where no one would search for them or even question why they suddenly had a third child. Back home, no one knew who had driven the other car, since it was reported stolen. Charles Junior had most likely stolen it on his night out with friends while drinking."

"This really has nothing to do with me..." Susan said and was about to get up from her seat. Jack signaled for her to sit down.

"How did you track him down? How did you find Benjamin? The Rutherfords had been very thorough and created a false identity for him with a social security number and everything."

Susan sank into her seat. Shannon sensed she was about to give up fighting this.

"I couldn't let it go. John, my husband, kept telling me to, but I couldn't. I was completely obsessed with finding him. It drove me nuts and almost ruined my marriage. I hired a private investigator to track the driver down, thinking that somehow Tommy, that was Benjamin's name before, had to have disappeared with him. It took the investigator almost four years and most of my savings, but he found the friends that Charles was out with that night and a neighbor who had seen him steal the car and recognized him as the pastor's son. But by then, they were long gone, and my husband got sick, so I let it go. Until he died and I didn't have any purpose in life anymore, at least that's how it felt. So, I found the old files again and started to look into them, then realized that the investigator had actually tracked the pastor down to living in Maggie Valley, North Carolina. So, I decided we should go there. I needed to get away; we both did."

"And you wanted to see your nephew," Jack said, sipping more coffee.

"It was this all-consuming mystery that I couldn't stop thinking about, no matter how much I tried. It was all day and all night, lurking in the back of my head. So finally, I had enough and decided to go. I didn't tell Savannah anything because she didn't need to know all this."

"You just hadn't expected her to fall for him," Jack said. "Nor had you expected to be pregnant with the pastor's baby. That's what derailed you, wasn't it? You were planning on destroying the family, getting close enough to them to find out everything you needed, then destroy them. That's why you started the affair with the pastor."

"I contacted Benjamin first. I went up to him in the parking lot outside the school and told him I knew who he was and that we were related. He hadn't met Savannah yet, and to this day, I still believe he only dated her to spite me. See, that was his character. He didn't want to reveal any of them and told me so when I tried to talk him into doing it. He told me he didn't need my help, that he was happy the way he was. How can you be happy this way? I asked him. Living a lie, never telling anyone who you really are?

"'This way, I get everything I want,' he said. Those were his words."

"And then he told me how he had made this flash drive many years ago, to blackmail his family. He used it to get his way in everything. That was how he got away with sleeping with his own sister, who wasn't his biological sister. Everyone believed she was the one obsessed with him, and she was, but only because he seduced her. He was the one who asked her to sleep with him; he was the one who told her that he would run away with her one day and they'd be an item. But he lied to her, thinking this family deserved no better for what they had done to his parents. Mr. and Mrs. Rutherford tried to stop him from ruining Penny's life, but he just told them that if they did, he'd reveal who he really was and send the proof to a journalist and the police. They'd all go to jail. Maybe not Penny, but the rest of them. Her, he only made believe he loved her, but the fact was that Benjamin loved no one but himself. He held them all prisoners and had them serving his every command and need. If ever anything happened to him, he'd have the proof sent out, and their lives would be over. He didn't want to destroy that. He had a great life this way, he told me. He didn't need my help. He started dating Savannah as protection. So, I wouldn't reveal anything. He knew I wouldn't want to risk hurting her."

"So, you came up with another way of hurting the Rutherfords and started an affair with the pastor," Jack said.

Susan sighed, then nodded. "I thought I could at least destroy what they had; I owed my sister that much. It wasn't like I'd have anything to lose."

"But then you fell for him, didn't you? Just like your daughter fell for Benjamin, and that screwed everything up, am I right? And with the baby coming and all, there really wasn't any part of you that wanted them to be revealed since the pastor would only end up in jail. He had promised you he'd leave his family for you, right?"

"Yes. He said he wanted to leave but was scared of what would happen. But then the strangest thing happened. A few days before he disappeared, Benjamin came to me and told me he was ready to tell. He was sick of his family and wanted them to finally get what they deserved. They had killed his parents and kidnapped him, and he wanted them to suffer for that. He was ready to tell. He knew a journalist who had been working on the story of the missing child from the crash for years, and she had offered him a great deal of money for an interview. He wanted me to know that he was coming clean, and he wanted me to support his story."

Susan sighed again and fiddled with her cup.

"And you told him you wouldn't do that, didn't you?" Jack asked. "You had come this far, but now you'd changed your mind."

Shannon held her breath as she watched the two of them, their eyes locked like two dogs ready to fight.

"Yes. I said I was over it and there was no need to do this anymore. I also begged him not to do it since I was pregnant with Charles' child and he had promised to leave his wife for me."

"And Benjamin told you he couldn't do that, right? He wanted the money that the journalist had promised him. He wanted them to hurt and then leave and begin a new life for himself. He knew they were getting tired of him and feared what they might do to him. He had gone too far."

Susan nodded.

"So, you killed him?"

73

M aggie Valley 2019
    January 25th
    11:36 PM

BENJAMIN WATCHED Savannah as she left the porch and got into her car. Their eyes locked once more before she drove off and disappeared into the night. Benjamin stood for a few seconds, looking after her, while Susan Kelsey watched him from her car. She had parked it at the neighboring cabin, waiting for her daughter to be done talking to him, and as soon as she drove away, Susan drove up into the driveway and parked. She grabbed the gun in her glove compartment and got out. She could still see Benjamin on the porch. The gun shook in her hands while she realized she wasn't completely clear about what her plan was. All she knew was that she was angry at Benjamin and she had to stop him somehow.

But Benjamin wasn't alone, she soon realized, and she hid behind the car to wait for this person to leave. As she looked up there, she realized he was talking to his brother in the wheelchair. They were fighting. Squatting behind the truck and listening, she could hear most of what they said. The voice speaking loudest was Benjamin's.

"You're a helpless idiot, you always have been, ever since that day. Why do you lurk in the darkness like this? Why do you listen in on my conversations, huh?"

"I was out here anyway," Charles Junior answered. "I didn't mean to eavesdrop. I'll go inside. You can deal with your own problems, and I will deal with mine, okay?"

"Problems? Problems, ha? I don't have any problems. Do you want to know why? Because I am not a liar or a kidnapper, that's why. You are all that and a murderer on top of it, and soon the entire world will know. They'll all know who and what you are, and you'll all get what you deserve."

"Please, Benjamin. Haven't we suffered enough for what we did? You've tortured us all for years, ever since you came with us. It was an accident. Don't you understand that? All we wanted was to move on and make sure you had a good life and a family to grow up in. We tried to give you a life. You'd have ended up in the foster care system if it wasn't for us. And all you have done is torture us."

"Well, get used to it, my friend, because you're in for a lot more suffering," he said, leaning close to his brother, breathing into his face. Charles Junior sobbed, bending his head down in shame.

Susan felt her heart knock against her rib cage. The gun felt heavy in her hand, and suddenly she regretted coming there. She felt like crying and put the gun in the back of her pants, then waited for a few seconds, waiting for them to go inside when suddenly she heard a loud thud, followed by a big bump. Startled, she peeked up above the front of the car and looked up at the porch. On the wooden floor, she saw Benjamin, his dead eyes staring accusatorily at her, blood running from the back of his head.

Susan gasped and clasped her mouth. And that was when they heard her.

"Who's there?" Mrs. Rutherford said and stepped into the sparse light. "Come forward, now!"

74

"So, it was Charles who hit him with the fire poker?" Shannon asked.

I shook my head as the final pieces fell into place. Susan was rubbing her fingers against each other nervously.

"It was Mrs. Rutherford, wasn't it?" I said.

Susan nodded. "Beatrice was still holding the fire poker in her gloved hands as I walked up there. She asked me if I had seen her do it. I said yes, but I also said I wouldn't tell if she didn't want me to. I guess I felt guilty somehow because of the affair and the pregnancy and all that. Plus, I was scared of her in that instant. She's a very frightening woman."

"So, you kept quiet for her sake?" Shannon said.

"I wanted him gone too, remember. Beatrice didn't need to say anything. Our eyes locked and we decided to help each other out. She couldn't lose her son. She couldn't lose Charles Junior, she kept saying. That was why she had done what she did back then, and that was why she did it again. I helped her carry the body to the freezer in the shack at the end of the property by the creek. The ground was too hard for us to dig a hole, and we knew the search teams would be out there when they realized he was gone in the morning, so we put him the freezer where there would be no smell for the hounds to find. Then we put the fire poker in the hatch and closed it. We had no idea Penny would find it all and think that Savannah had placed it there. Their uncle had heard everything and came out to help us carry the body away. Beatrice made him swear never to tell anyone, but then he did anyway. While drunk, he spoke to that journalist who was still on the story after Benjamin had talked to her. She knew everything, and now that Benjamin was gone, she suddenly started to dig deeper, realizing that there was a huge story in there somewhere. She knew something had happened to Benjamin and wouldn't believe that he had just run off. She met with the uncle in a bar, got him plastered, and then he blabbed. Soon, she found the horse wrangler, and he revealed that he had been working late that night and then come out of the stables just in time to see us carry the body away. Lyle Bishop was in the house when it happened because he was dating Penny at the time and must have seen it happen since he was also talking to the journalist. Back when Savannah showed me the flash drive, I told her to forget all about it. If the police ever questioned her, she was supposed to not talk about it. I said it was a matter of life and death. It would ruin everything if she mentioned it. She didn't know anything. She had left before it happened, so she didn't know who killed Benjamin. But she had seen what was on the flash drive. She knew their secret. I explained to her why I had asked her to keep quiet about it when she got out of jail. I told her I was in love with the pastor and the information on the flash drive could hurt him. Then she ran off and well...you know the rest better than I do."

"Why did you fight with him?" Shannon asked. "I saw you two fighting in the parking lot."

"He was going to back out. He couldn't leave Beatrice now that they had lost their son, he said, and then he got very aggressive, trying to get me to leave him alone. But it started before Benjamin went missing. As soon as I told him about the pregnancy, that's when everything changed. I was mad at him for some time for reacting that way. I think he got scared. Maybe he did love his wife after all and didn't want to lose her. I don't think he knew that Beatrice had killed Benjamin, but I think he suspected that she might have. He was afraid of what was going to happen. Would Beatrice tell the police everything? Would it be revealed somehow anyway that they had taken Benjamin and that Charles Junior had killed those two people on the day of the accident? I never heard him say these things, but that's what I assume he was thinking after I read the stuff on the flash drive. Anyway, I don't care anymore. Beatrice killed my daughter and, to be honest, I want her to fry for what she's done. She shot her that night on the ledge. My guess is she knew that Savannah had the flash drive and that's why she had to die. No one could know. She couldn't risk that Savannah spoke to anyone about it. I guess it was my fault since I told her to keep quiet when talking to the police. If she had just told them, we wouldn't be sitting here. The Rutherfords would have been revealed and jailed for their acts. And my Savannah would be..."

Susan stopped and sniffled. She wiped her nose on a tissue and shook her head.

"How do you know it was Mrs. Rutherford?" I asked. "How do you know she shot Savannah?"

Susan lifted her glare, and our eyes met across the room. I sensed deep anger but also regret in them.

"She was an army sniper. Took three trips to Iraq back in the nineties. I've been up to that place after I was told what happened to Savannah. I saw what distance she made the shot from, and at night-time on top of it. To my knowledge, she's the only one around here who can shoot like that."

75

"Come on, Austin! Come play with us."

Abigail bent down and gathered enough snow to shape a ball and throw it at her brother. It landed a few feet from where he was sitting. Abigail yelled his name again and signaled for him to join them, but Austin shook his head. He didn't want to play in the snow with his siblings. He didn't feel like it. He felt cold and awful. His father had ended up in the hospital, and it was all his fault. If only he had told him what he knew, then all of this wouldn't have happened. But how could he have? When he knew he risked all their lives if he did?

Austin shook his head. It didn't matter anymore. As soon as his dad came back from the hospital later today, he was going to tell him everything. It was about time.

"Austin, come on!"

Abigail yelled at the top of her lungs just as Angela threw a snowball at her and hit her forehead. Abigail shrieked as snow slid into her eyes.

"I'm gonna get you for this!" she yelled joyfully, then threw herself on top of Angela. They landed in the snow and started laughing, rolling around.

Tyler and Betsy Sue were building an igloo, or what was supposed to be one, piling up snow in the middle of the yard. Tyler waddled in his snowsuit while gathering snow between his hands and putting it on top of the mountain, while Betsy Sue began hollowing it.

Austin kicked the snow in front of him, annoyed. He missed being able to have fun like his siblings, and he envied his twin sister for being able to always make the best of any situation, of always finding joy even when things were tough.

Abigail ran across the yard, trying to get away from Angela, when she tripped and fell onto the igloo, missing Betsy Sue's head by only a few inches.

"Hey!" Betsy Sue yelled when Abigail landed in the middle of her pile with a loud laugh.

"Hey!" Tyler chimed in, placing his hands on his sides.

Abigail couldn't stop laughing, and Tyler grabbed a big pile of snow and placed it on top of her. Seconds later, they all threw themselves in the soft white powder and started making snow angels.

Tired of watching them, Austin rose to his feet. He walked in between the tall trees till he reached the creek. He bent down and stared into the crackling water, seeing his own reflection, then sighed. He reached his hand into the water and felt the freezing cold hit the tips of his fingers. As he pulled it out with a light gasp, he saw something in the reflection in front of him. A face and a set of eyes that made him wet his pants. Austin tried to scream, but a hand placed in front of his mouth blocked out all sound.

76

I spotted the kids playing in the yard as soon as we drove up in the driveway. The sight of them making snow angels made me smile. It was late in the afternoon, and we had spent way too long at Susan's place. We had talked and talked and finally called the sheriff. He had arrived with a couple of deputies, and Susan had told them her story once again, crying heavily this time. We had left, leaving the sheriff to deal with the rest. Hopefully, they would arrest Mrs. Rutherford within the next few hours, but I wasn't going to meddle anymore. I was just happy I wasn't working the case since it was quite the mess to figure out the details. But luckily, it was someone else's mess. All I wanted was to be with my family and hopefully enjoy the rest of my vacation. I knew I wasn't going to be able to snowboard anymore while there, but at least I could get to be with my most favorite people in the world.

Shannon parked the car in front of the cabin, and I got out, leaning on my cane. Abigail was the first to spot me.

"Daaaaaad!"

She ran to me and threw herself at me, hugging me tightly.

"Easy there, Abigail," Shannon said. "He's still in a lot of pain."

"Are you, Daddy?" she said, her big blue eyes looking up at me. Those eyes just about made my heart stop.

I chuckled and kissed the top of her head. "I'm getting better."

The other kids came up behind Abigail, Tyler waddling, then tripping and falling flat on his face in the snow. Shannon ran to help him up. Tyler wailed as his face emerged from the snow, and Shannon kissed his red cheeks. As soon as he saw me, the tears stopped, and he remembered his mission. I reached out my one arm that wasn't leaning on the cane and grabbed him from Shannon. He hugged me tightly.

"Say, have you grown?" I asked. "You feel heavier, and you look a lot taller than when I last saw you."

Tyler's face lit up. There was nothing he wanted more in the world than to be as tall as his siblings. He hugged me again, then grew tired of being held and squirmed to let me know he wanted to get down. I put him down, and he waddled off, while Betsy Sue and Angela came up to me.

"I am so glad you're back," Angela said and hugged me. I looked into her eyes and realized she was growing into looking like her mother more and more each day. She was going to be quite the looker, that one, but then again, all my girls were beautiful. Even Betsy Sue who had reached that awkward puberty age with all the hormone pimples spreading across her cheeks and forehead. To me, she was still the most beautiful girl in the world. It was all in her eyes. I hugged her too, and she hurried away shyly, the way she always did. I looked behind the kids, then around us.

"Where's Austin?"

I looked at his sister when asking, and she shrugged. "I don't know. How am I supposed to know?"

"He wasn't playing with you out here?" I asked.

Abigail shook her head. "He was out here just a moment ago, watching us, but he didn't want to play. He just sat there, all angry and stuff. Like he has been all week."

"Maybe he went back inside," Shannon said and started walking toward the porch, where Bridget now came out.

"Welcome back, Mr. Ryder," she said, taking off her glasses. In her hand, she was holding a book. She kept a finger placed inside of it, keeping her on the page she had reached.

"Thank you. Do you have Austin inside with you?" I asked, feeling anxious.

She looked puzzled. "Well, no. I sent them all outside to play, thinking a little fresh air would do them good. I've been watching them through the window while reading."

77

"AUSTIN!"

I limped around the house while calling his name, panic rushing through me. Shannon went inside the house and seconds later she came back out, holding a stack of papers in her hand.

"Jack, come look at this."

I was standing in the area behind the house where Abigail had told me she had last seen him sitting. I looked around me, not seeing any trace of him. Shannon walked up to me and showed the papers to me. They were drawings, Austin's drawings.

"I think you need to take a look at these," she said.

I stared at the pictures my son had been drawing for the past few days and felt my heart drop. All of them showed the scene at the ski school. A lot of them were mostly black and red, but it was still very easy to tell what was going on, and exactly what had happened. The realization hit me like a punch in the stomach.

"How did we not see this earlier?" Shannon asked, clasping her mouth. "I mean, I watched him while he drew, but I never really looked at them, you know? I never really saw what it was he was drawing. I tried to get him to express himself through music, to get whatever he was carrying out through singing when all the time he used his skills at drawing. This was his outlet, and we failed to see it. All this time the answer was right there."

"And because he was told not to tell anyone, he thought he couldn't, that we would all get killed if he did," I said. "So, he drew instead. He drew what we needed to know. If only we had seen this sooner."

"I can't believe it," Shannon said.

I looked at the neighboring house, anger rising in my throat when my phone buzzed in my pocket. I picked it up and looked at the display. I had received a text from an unknown number. I opened it.

THE GHOST TOWN. COME ALONE, OR HE DIES.

"God, no," I said and read it again, my heart pounding in my chest.

"What is it, Jack?" Shannon said. "What's going on?"

I swallowed, and our eyes met. It was getting darker out, and soon the sun would set behind the mountains, leaving us all in darkness. I had to find Austin before that happened. He had to be terrified.

"I...I have to go. Can you look after the kids?"

"What's going on, Jack?"

"I can't tell you." I stared at her, debating within whether or not to let her in on what I had received in the text. But I didn't want her to know more since she would only demand that I involve the police, and right now, I didn't dare to. But, of course, she already suspected.

"Call the sheriff, Jack, please. Take them with you."

I shook my head. "I can't. I have to do this alone."

"That's not a good idea, Jack, not in your condition," Shannon said as I walked toward the car. "Jack?"

"I have to go."

"Jack...you just got out of the hospital. You can barely walk on your own, and this...it could get really dangerous."

I shook my head and opened the door to the car, then got in. "I have to do it, Shannon. I have to. I'm sorry."

78

Austin didn't know where he was. A cloth had been stuffed into his mouth and made it hard for him to breathe properly. He had been blindfolded and tied up. Now he was put down in a seat somewhere. The chair he was sitting in was hard, and he could feel the fresh cold air on his face, which meant he was still outdoors.

Austin whimpered behind the cloth as he felt the person's hands let go of him and place his hands on something cold, something that felt like steel. He was crying and wanted to scream but couldn't.

Dad? Where are you? I wanna go home now. Please.

"There you are," the person said. "All ready."

The sound of the person's voice made Austin shiver. He remembered it vividly from that day at the ski school just as he remembered those eyes that had looked at him before telling him to keep quiet. Those burning eyes with such menace in them it had frightened Austin to silence.

Please, let me go. I won't tell anyone. I never did. I promise I won't.

Austin felt the tears roll down his cheek and grow cold on his skin. A breeze hit his face, and he shivered. Where was he? It felt so cold, and the wind was so harsh on his skin.

"There, there. No need to be crying," the person said and wiped away one of the tears that slid under the blindfold. "Daddy will be here soon, and then you'll be reunited again. In death."

As the person said the words, Austin gasped behind the gag. He screamed but nothing but muffled sounds left his throat, and he felt like he was choking. He wanted to yell; he wanted to scream at his dad to stay away, to not come there, but he couldn't. Instead, he let more tears escape his eyes and turned his head in the direction of where he thought he heard the person's voice coming from. It was suddenly a lot farther away.

"Get ready, my sweet boy, you're in for quite the ride."

As the words fell, the sound of an engine turning on drowned out everything else. It hissed and coughed before finally coming to life, and the next thing Austin knew, he was moving fast through the freezing air, music blasting in his ears.

79

The chairlift was running when I reached the entrance to Ghost Town in the Sky. The lights were turned on, running up the mountainside like glowing pearls on a string, lighting up the entire forest surrounding it.

I parked the car outside the building and stared up at the top of Buck Mountain, where the chairlift ended. I exhaled, then leaned over and grabbed my gun out of the glove compartment. Shannon didn't know it was in there since she hated the thought of guns being even near her and especially the children. She was terrified that one of them would get ahold of it and accidentally shoot themselves or their siblings, so I kept it in a gun case that only my fingerprints could open.

I placed the gun in the back of my pants and got out, leaning on my cane, I headed toward the lifts. As I sat down on the chair, I felt a rush of anxiety roll over me, fearing for what waited for me once I got up there. I placed the cane on my side and touched the gun briefly to make sure it was still there. I kept my hand on it till the chair approached the top, and I had to get off.

I almost tripped when I jumped down to the ground and landed on my bad leg, but by placing the cane in the snow, I prevented my fall. I got up properly and looked ahead into the street going through the old Wild West town. With the moon shining down from above me, I could see most of the houses going down the street.

I passed the old Silver Dollar Saloon and a shop where the sign said OLD TYME PHOTOS and the Golden Nugget Casino. The Mad Hatter shop had lost a couple of letters in its sign and just read THE M D HAT R. The Pack Mule Giftshop still had little trinkets in the windows.

I had one hand on my cane, the other on the gun behind my back as I walked slowly down the small street. As I walked further, something caught my attention. It was a sound, the sound of music frantically playing from somewhere behind the houses.

Carousel music.

What in the...?

I sprang forward, the best I could in my condition, and walked between two of the old wooden houses when I saw the lit-up roller coaster where the music was playing.

It was turned on, and the small wagons were rushing through the many turns and loops. The empty carts, along with the frenzied music, made it so eerie the hairs rose on the back of my neck. As I approached the sign where it said: RED DEVIL CLIFFHANGER, I soon realized that not all the wagons were empty. Inside one of them, I spotted someone as it rushed past me, a gust of wind making my hair rise on top of my head. Someone was sitting in the front wagon all alone.

A little boy.

"AUSTIN!"

I walked closer, heart hammering in my chest with worry. Austin hated roller coasters more than anyone since he was terrified of heights and he always got sick to his stomach when riding one.

"Austin!"

I hurried toward what looked like a small control house, thinking

I might be able to stop the roller coaster in there when the sound of a shot being fired crashed through the crisp air.

I ducked down, heart pounding in my throat, and looked in the direction from where the sound was coming when I realized the shooter wasn't aiming at me.

They were shooting at Austin sitting in the roller coaster.

80

The wagons rushed past me again, sending off another gust of air into my face. I wanted to scream as another shot was fired and I heard the bullet ricochet off the side of the wagon. I ducked down not to get hit as it bounced off and hit a tree behind me.

I looked up at the rooftop of one of the old western houses and spotted movement. I couldn't really see what it was in the darkness but felt convinced it had to be the shooter.

Another shot was fired as the wagon once again passed me, and I screamed. I grabbed my gun and lifted it, aiming it toward the rooftop, but then realized I couldn't see well enough. I wondered if I could find my way into the control house and stop the roller coaster but then realized that if the wagon stood still, it would be even easier for the shooter to hit my son. As long as he was moving, it was harder. I also realized that it was probably what the shooter wanted me to do. To try and stop Austin and get to him, and then he would shoot us both.

I rose to my feet and rushed to the house as yet another shot was fired, and my heart almost stopped. As I stared helplessly at the racing wagon, I couldn't see if my son was dead or still alive, and that made me rush to find the stairs on the side of the building. I hurried up there, using my cane to jolt me upward and soon I was on the flat roof, walking closer to the shooter who was lying at the edge, the rifle placed on the ground. My fingers clasped the gun, and I held it out in front of me, ready to make an end of it.

The shooter reloaded and aimed.

"Come one step closer, and your son dies," the voice said.

"He's moving fast," I said, pointing the gun at the shooter. "How will you make sure you hit him before I shoot you?"

"Did you know I used to be a biathlete?" he said, still following my son through the scope. "The sport where you combine cross country skiing with rifle shooting."

"I know what biathlon is," I said.

"Good, then you might also know that it's a sport with roots in old hunting techniques that have been used in Scandinavian countries for centuries. Hunters searched for prey using skis, their rifles attached to their backs. That is also how I trained for my contests...by shooting deer and even smaller animals. You might also know that in a contest, missed shots result in extra distance or time being added to the contest's total. I represented our proud nation in the winter Olympics in Salt Lake in '02 and won gold, the first ever American medal in biathlon because of my shooting. I am a very steady shooter; I never miss if I don't want to. I can shoot anything, even when moving. A moving target is just more fun. Gives me a challenge, you know?"

"That was before you became a pastor, I take it," I said.

"It most certainly was," Charles Rutherford said. "Put the gun down, or the kid dies. I have only been having fun with him so far, but I can make it happen in a matter of seconds if you don't do as I say."

I stared at the roller coaster, then down at the pastor. Remembering how great of a shot he had been when I had tried to escape him on the ledge, I didn't dare take the risk. I put the gun down on the roof.

"There. Now leave my son alone."

"Kick it over here."

I did as he told me to while the wagon rushed past us in the distance once more, and I wondered if Austin was still alive inside of it.

The pastor looked up at me. "You don't seem surprised. When did you realize I was the one you were looking for?"

I swallowed. "My son's drawings. He drew you at the ski school on the day you shot and killed Lyle Bishop. Up until then, I was certain it was your wife. She did, after all, kill Benjamin."

"Only to protect her family. She is not a killer. She only did what was necessary, and so did I. She's the one I'm protecting now," he said. "She's my wife. It's my family you're threatening to destroy. It's what families do; we protect each other, no matter what. No matter the cost. She made me realize that. She told me everything when that reporter started snooping around. I told her to calm down and that I would clean up the mess. I decided at that moment that nothing would ever break us apart again."

"That's why you killed everyone who had talked to Eliza and tried to get rid of her too? But it kept adding up. The number of people who knew what was going on kept growing, and so you had to kill more. It wouldn't stop. You even had to kill a seventeen-year-old girl who had done nothing wrong, the sister of your unborn child. You had hoped she'd kill herself, now that everyone hated her, but she didn't, so you decided to help her along, am I right?"

"I thought the text would make her jump over the edge, so to speak. But then you jumped in after her and saved her, and I had to finish the job. If you hadn't fallen off the ledge, I would have gotten you as well. I knew if I shot you, they wouldn't have found you till spring if they ever found you. Animals would have eaten most of your bodies."

"But why were you so keen on protecting your family? You were the one who was about to destroy it anyway, with Susan being pregnant and all."

The pastor grumbled. "That was a mistake. She was a mistake. It should never have happened. I was weak for a minute, and that got me in trouble. It won't happen again. Beatrice and I found each other again in this, once we both confessed everything to each other. Beatrice came to me when she realized that the journalist was snooping around. She told me what had happened that night and how she had gotten so mad, finally having enough of the boy, she had knocked him out with the fire poker. She told me how he had constantly threatened to reveal her little secret if she didn't do as he told her...if she didn't let him have sex with...with our daughter. Can you imagine having to go through something like that as a parent? It was torture for us. We could just see how it was destroying our sweet Penelope, how her infatuation with Benjamin was consuming her. It was about to crush her. And all we could do was watch.

Meanwhile, he ran around dating that other girl, Savannah and made a complete fool out of Penny. Beatrice didn't plan on killing him. She simply had enough when she heard how he threatened our son out on the porch after Savannah had left that night. She couldn't take anymore, and she lost it. On that same night as she confessed all this to me, I also told her about my affair with Susan and the child she was expecting. We agreed to clean up our messes. I would get rid of anyone who posed a threat to us. The plan was to make it look like suicide, so no one could trace it back to us. We promised each other not to let anyone come between us again."

"So, you planned on getting rid of Susan too, but you couldn't get yourself to kill her since she was carrying your child."

"I told her to leave town. I even tried to pay her to go. But she refused. She had this idea that we could be together. She begged me to leave Beatrice. I finally explained to her that it was over and that my family means everything to me."

"Meanwhile, you were all busy blaming her daughter, Savannah," I said, "especially Charles Junior, who lied to my wife and told her Savannah had been aggressive toward both him and Benjamin on the night he disappeared. But your wife, Mrs. Rutherford, didn't want you accusing Savannah. She believed she owed Susan for helping her on the day she killed Benjamin, or maybe she was just afraid that Susan would reveal everything if her daughter was accused of murder. But Susan is done keeping your secrets. She's talking to the sheriff right now. She told me everything about that night, and now she's agreed to tell him too. You both relied on her to remain silent, but she won't keep quiet any more. Not after you killed Savannah, the only one she had left to protect. As we speak, they're probably coming for your wife and son."

Pastor Rutherford didn't move.

"It's over," I said.

He shook his head with a sniffle. "Not till I say so."

The pastor looked into the scope, then fired a shot, then another. My heart stopped as I heard the bullets whistle through the air, not knowing if any of them hit my son. As I turned to look, tears springing to my eyes, the pastor had picked up my gun and pointed it at me.

In the moonlight, I could see his lips peel off his teeth in a smile. Then he pulled the trigger.

81

I stared at the gun in the pastor's hand. His eyes were wide in the sparse moonlight, his mouth gaping. I gasped and felt my stomach, but much to my surprise, I felt no blood, and I was in no pain.

What happened?

As I slowly started to breathe again, gasping for air, I realized I wasn't the one who had been hit. The pastor gurgled and dropped the gun, then clasped his chest, and that was when I saw it. Blood was gushing out from a bullet wound. The pastor tried to speak, but nothing came out, and soon he collapsed. His limp body landed on the rooftop with a thud, while my heart raced in my chest. I turned to look behind me and spotted someone standing there. As he approached me, I recognized him.

It was Douglas Rutherford, the pastor's brother.

"Charles!" he yelled and ran to his brother's body. He knelt next to him and lifted his head into his lap. He rocked him back and forth, crying. The pastor remained lifeless. He was dead.

"I am so sorry. I am so, so sorry, brother."

He looked at me, and I exhaled.

"I had to stop him," Douglas said, sobbing. "He was going to kill you."

"I...I..."

I tried to speak, but I couldn't really find the words. I still couldn't quite believe I wasn't the one lying there in a pool of my own blood. I had been so certain this was the end.

"He was the good one, you know?" Douglas said. "I was the black sheep. I was the one who was supposed to be lying there. He tried to kill me. He came to the shack and tried to shoot me, but I escaped. I hid for days till I realized I had to act. I knew what they had been up to. I saw Beatrice kill Benjamin. I even helped her and that other woman carry the dead body to the freezer, while Charles Junior just watched us. I also knew that my brother Charles killed the stable guy and Lyle Bishop. I knew what they had done to Benjamin, stealing him so he would never talk. I knew everything, yet I kept quiet. I was a drunk. Who would ever believe me? I kept asking myself. But that was just a lousy excuse. Fact was, I was a coward. I didn't dare stand up to my own brother. I should have told him it was wrong when he told me about Charles Junior's accident and taking the boy. That was when I should have taken my stand. But I didn't, and then suddenly the ball was rolling. One lie became a lot more just to cover up that first one, and soon I was just as guilty as they were. I even went so far that I cleaned the darn freezer out to cover for them after I saw you coming out of there. But then he wanted to kill me. Me, who had been loyal to him for all those years. Because I got drunk and told. One stupid night when I couldn't keep it in anymore. I managed to get away, and I think he thought I was dead. After he tried to kill me, I was done with keeping their secrets. I went there to tell him. I wanted to give him the chance to tell the truth himself, so I went to his house. I didn't come unprotected this time. I broke into a cabin where I found the rifle and brought it with me in case he tried anything again. I went there to confront him, but as I got there, I saw him with that kid by the creek. I watched from between the trees as he grabbed him and ran away with him. I followed him here, and that's when you showed up. It took me a while to gather the courage to stop him. But now, I have. Once and for all."

I was breathing easier now. I looked at him, then placed a hand on his shoulder.

"For what it's worth, thank you."

He sniffled and looked down at his brother. "Those that said better late than never weren't really in this type of situation, were they?"

"Still, you saved my life."

I said the words while dialing nine-one-one. Clutching the phone against my ear and talking to the dispatcher, telling her to send help, I climbed down the stairs and ran as fast as possible while still supported by the cane. I rushed toward the roller coaster.

"How many?" the dispatcher asked. "How many ambulances? How many are hurt?"

I found the control room and found the big STOP button and pressed it. The carousel music died, and the roller-coaster stopped abruptly.

"Sir? How many are hurt?"

I swallowed as I spotted my son in the front wagon, hunched forward. He wasn't moving. I ran to him, while the woman on the other end grew impatient.

"Sir? Sir?"

I grabbed my son and pulled him upright, my heart knocking violently against my ribcage.

Please, let him be alive, God. Please.

As I touched my son, I felt my hand get sticky, and I looked at him with a loud gasp. Tears sprang to my eyes as the woman yelled at the other end.

"Sir. Are you still there? Hello? Sir?"

I took a deep breath, forcing myself to calm down as I reached over and grabbed my son, pulling him out of the seat, crying desperately. I dropped the phone into the snow when Austin was finally in my arms, and I slid to the ground, holding him tight, his blood soaking my jacket.

"Sir? Sir? How many people are hurt? Please, sir?"

I held my son close and spoke through a curtain of tears.

"TWO. Two people have been shot!"

82

It was the longest night of my life. I waited in the hospital for news about Austin, and Shannon came to be with me. She had gotten Bridget to keep an eye on the kids, so I didn't have to be alone. We held each other tight all night while Austin was in surgery, and in the morning, Bridget brought all the kids to us. Abigail climbed into my lap and curled up like a small ball, crying.

"Please, tell me he'll make it," she said. "Please, Daddy."

I had never seen her like this. Usually, Abigail always found some way to keep positive and make the best of any moment, but this was her twin brother, the one she had shared every moment of her life with, even in her mother's womb. She had never known life without him.

Shannon brought me coffee while Abigail curled up in my embrace. I took it and drank it, wondering how I could have been so stupid. How had I missed Austin's drawings? How had I not even thought about looking at them? Especially when he had refused to talk. I should have known that this was how he'd communicate about things he couldn't talk about. Him being in there, on that surgery table, was all my fault.

Shannon saw how tormented I was and leaned over to kiss me. She looked into my eyes.

"You can go all the way back to deciding to come on this trip," she said, "if you want to find more ways to blame yourself for this. I mean, it was your idea, right? To go skiing."

I exhaled. "It's hard not to."

She shook her head and kissed me again. "Don't do this to yourself. It's not doing you any good. It's not even helping Austin."

A tear escaped my eye and Shannon wiped it away with her thumb.

"I can't lose him, Shannon. I simply can't. I will never be able to forgive myself."

"At least you solved the case," Shannon said. "Beatrice Rutherford is in jail, and so is her son."

I sighed. "It's not much of a consolation. I just want my son back. I just want to go home with my son."

Shannon sighed and grabbed my hand in hers. "I know. I know."

I leaned my head back till it touched the wall behind me. I was getting sick of sitting in these uncomfortable chairs. I didn't even know how long I had been there.

"Why don't they say anything?" I asked. "It's been so many hours."

"They will," Shannon said. "They're probably just busy, you know?"

"You should have seen him, Shannon. When they rushed him off down the hallway and told me to stay behind. I almost lost it. My little boy with all those people and tubes and the doctors were yelling and rolling him away. It almost broke me, Shannon. What if that was the last time I saw him alive? I can't stand the thought."

"How bad was it?" she asked, her watchful eye constantly on Tyler, who had started exploring the waiting room.

"He had lost a lot of blood. I tried to wake him up while we waited for the helicopter to get him, but he was completely lifeless. The longest minutes of my life. I was so scared, Shannon."

Shannon squeezed my hand as the door suddenly opened, and a man in blue scrubs entered. The front of his suit had blood on it, and I wondered if it was my son's. He took off his mask and looked at us, a serious look in his eyes.

"Mr. Ryder?"

83

"The projectile entered the patient on the right side of his chest. There's severe damage to the tissue, shattered bone, and damaged nerves. Luckily, it seems that no heart venous or arterial vessels are fractured. Now, the right lung was damaged, and that is the serious part. There is a great risk for pneumothorax, a collapse of the lung, but for now, we seem to be in the clear as we have reestablished the pressure in his lung and inserted a chest tube. This will continuously remove air from the chest cavity until his lung is healed. His ribs were shattered when the projectile entered his body, and the splinters themselves have been cutting into blood vessels and arteries surrounding them. We have spent all night removing those splinters."

Shannon glanced quickly at Jack. He was listening with his eyes wide open, and she could tell he was trying to understand what was being said, but not succeeding very well. She couldn't blame him. She had a gazillion thoughts in her mind too, and it had to be a lot worse for him.

"But what does it mean, Doctor?" she asked, trying to help him out. "Is Austin...?"

The doctor nodded. "He's alive, yes, and stable for now. But he needs to be monitored closely. The next twenty-four hours will be crucial for his chances of survival. We can't say anything with certainty yet, but as I said, he is stable for now. We'll let you know if anything changes in his condition and update you as often as we can. But I need you to be patient. Okay?"

"Thank you, Doctor," Shannon said and grabbed Jack by the shoulders as the doctor disappeared back out the same door that he had entered a few minutes earlier. Jack stood motionless and stared at the doors.

"It was good news, Jack," she said, trying to get him to look her in the eyes. "Austin is alive. Now, all we have to do is wait."

Jack lifted his eyes, and her heart dropped when she saw the look in them. He shook his head.

"Come here. Sit down," she said and guided him to a chair. She sat next to him and took his hands in hers. "He's not in the clear yet, but he's stable. He will get better, Jack. I know he will."

Jack exhaled and leaned back in the chair, letting his head rest on the wall behind him, covering his face with his hands while groaning. Tyler crawled into his lap and sat there, looking up at his dad with a big smile. When Jack bent his head back down, the boy handed him something, and Jack looked at what it was. An old smeared chocolate bar that Shannon had no idea how he had gotten ahold of. He hadn't even opened it but kept it in his hand where it had almost melted.

"I am sorry, Jack," she said and reached for the bar. "I'll get you a new one from the vending machine outside."

Jack moved his hand with the bar in it so she couldn't reach it. Then he laughed. Tears streamed across his cheeks, and he leaned over and kissed his son on the top of his head.

"This is the best present I ever got. How did you know, buddy? How did you know that this was just what I needed?"

Tyler smiled from ear to ear, then pointed at his head. "Magic."

Jack chortled and pulled the boy into a deep embrace while the tears kept rolling. Shannon watched the two of them while bracing herself for having to go through yet another twenty-four hours of despairing uncertainty.

84

Exactly thirty hours later, they finally gave us the all-clear. The doctor from earlier came out and told us Austin was no longer in critical condition and that he was awake.

"You can go see him now," he said.

Never have I rushed so fast, heart throbbing in my chest, the cane clacking against the floor as I hurried down the hallway.

"Austin? Austin?"

Panic erupted in my voice as I finally found his room and pulled away the curtain.

"Austin?"

There he was. My little boy, lying in that awful bed surrounded by machines, his small blue eyes lingering on me. I saw such sorrow in them; I could barely take it.

"Austin?" I said and approached him. He reached out his hand, and I took it, pressing it against my cheek, tears gushing from my eyes. "Oh, Austin, I was so scared."

"I...I'm sorry, Daddy," his small hoarse voice whispered. "I...I should have..."

"No," I said, cutting him off. "I am not going to let you blame yourself for this. I am the one who didn't see; I am the one who was blind."

Austin smiled wearily. He was so pale I could hardly recognize him. He coughed and I could tell speaking was tough on him. A tube still helped him breathe. He was going to have to stay at the hospital for the next two weeks, according to the doctor. I was going to stay with him until he was fully recovered. I was never leaving his side again.

"Finally, you're awake, doofus," Abigail said and came up to him. She too seemed weak and out of it. Her eyes were blank, and I could tell she had feared losing him.

Austin gave her a feeble smile as their eyes met, and I felt that deep connection that only the two of them had. It was a twin-thing, a doctor had once explained to me. They connected on a deeper level than any of us ever would. I sighed with relief, thinking there was no way Abigail could have made it had Austin died. In their eyes, there were only the two of them and then the rest of the world. One didn't exist without the other.

"How are you feeling, Austin?" Angela asked as she came up to him. Angela had had a crush on him ever since I met Shannon and their lives were brought together. A tear escaped her eye, and she wiped it away. He lifted his hand and signaled for her to take it. They held hands for a few seconds, while Tyler crawled up on the bed and handed Austin a flat chocolate granola bar.

"Seriously? Where does he get them from?" Shannon asked, startled.

That made all of us laugh. It wasn't even that funny, but I guess we needed a good laugh more than anything at this point.

EPILOGUE

Two days before they released Austin, I bumped into Deputy Winston by the vending machine in the hallway. I had been living off bars and sodas for almost two weeks now. Shannon and the kids had decided to go back and get the kids to school before they missed too much important stuff. Meanwhile, I had stayed at the hospital, sleeping in a chair, not letting my boy out of my sight. Austin was improving rapidly, the doctor told me, and would probably recover fully in time. But he needed to take it easy for a few more weeks once we got back. Meanwhile, I had finally lost the cane and was walking almost normally now.

"Hello there, Detective," Winston said.

"Deputy? What brings you here?"

"You didn't hear? Eliza Reuben woke up. The sheriff and I just spoke to her, got her statement. Everything she told us supported your story. It was the pastor she had faced in Harry Mayer's house when finding his dead body and trying to resuscitate him, and it was also him who followed her in the black truck, chasing her until she crashed. Too bad the laptop in her briefcase was destroyed by the impact. She said she had recorded interviews with all of them on it, but she also said she uploaded them all to a drop box, that she always does that in case something happens, and she'll try to access it as soon as possible. Fingers crossed that it'll work since that will give us the last evidence we need for our case against Beatrice Rutherford and her son Charles Junior. We want to put both of them away for a very long time."

"Sounds good," I said.

"Say, how's that boy of yours doing? He any better?"

I nodded, feeling confident that it was all going to be good again. I opened my granola bar with peanut butter and took a bite.

"He will be. I'll be taking him home in two days."

"That's good," Winston said. "Don't reckon we'll be seeing any of you back here next year."

I chuckled and chewed. "Probably not. Might want to go someplace warm next time. I've always wanted to go surfing in Puerto Rico."

Winston nodded and shook my hand. "Well, it was nice to meet you, Detective. Take care now."

"You too."

I stared after Winston as he left, then continued down the hallway past Austin's room, where he was sound asleep, and stopped in front of another room. I knocked gently and waited for the response.

"Come in."

I peeked inside and smiled. She returned my smile.

"I know who you are. I saw your picture in my paper," she said and held a copy of The Mountaineer up. They had been writing about the case consistently since it was revealed that it was his own mother who had killed Benjamin, or rather the woman everyone believed was his mother. The last I had read, they had written that, after her release, Benjamin's sister, Penny, had gone up north to live with her aunt, Ginger Rutherford, who was apparently some famous author. The media had been on top of one another to get a statement from the girl, but she had refused to give one, and her aunt had instead pleaded with them to give the family some peace to recover. Penny had admitted to having been the one who attacked Colette, trying to get her to stop seeing Benjamin, but Colette had decided not to press charges, and so she was free to go. Douglas Rutherford, the uncle, had admitted to helping hide the body of Benjamin and was facing accessory charges.

I stepped closer.

"Thanks for the flowers," she said. "And—oh, yeah—for saving my life."

I shrugged. "No problem."

"It's good finally to have a face for the famous Detective Ryder," she said. "The man who saved me and solved the case."

"Cost me dearly, though," I said and threw away the wrapper in the bin by the sink.

Her eyes grew serious. "I heard about your son. Will he be okay?"

I nodded and swallowed, then wiped my hands on my pants. I had worn the same clothes for days and felt so sticky it was disgusting.

"They seem to think so, yes."

She exhaled. "Oh, good. I am glad. Awful story."

"You can say that again. Anyway, I just wanted to say hello to you properly. I feel like I know you."

"Same here. Say, speaking of story, would you dare to tell yours?" she asked. "And feel free to say no if you don't want to. I won't be offended. You don't owe me anything. It's the other way around."

"You mean like an interview?"

She sighed and nodded. "I would like to tell the entire story of what happened to Benjamin Rutherford and how it was solved—told through the eyes of the detective who put the pieces together, through lots of difficulty. I actually think it might make a book. Could end up making you famous. What do you say?"

I looked at the woman sitting in her bed. "You journalists never sleep, do you?"

"Well, I just woke up from a pretty long nap, so I think I'll be good for a little while."

I looked into her eyes while thinking it over, then shook my head when thinking about my family. A project like this could end up taking an enormous amount of time, and I didn't have that with five children in the house under the age of thirteen and a wife who loved her job and would probably soon get back to the stage. I was needed at home and, to be honest, that was exactly where I wanted to be. I already had a famous wife and had seen how it complicated her life, our life together. We didn't need any more of that.

"You know what?" I said. "I think I'll pass on that one."

She nodded. "I had a feeling you might say that. Family comes first; I take it?"

I smiled and opened the door to her room.

"Exactly."

THE END

AFTERWORD

Dear Reader,

Thank you for purchasing *Don't Tell* (Jack Ryder #7). This story came to life when one of my loyal readers contacted me and asked me if I had ever heard about the story of Ella Maud Cropsey (or often known as just Nell Cropsey).

It was the story of a young girl who disappeared from the porch of her family home in North Carolina in November 1901 after a fight with her boyfriend.

This reader was related to Nell and was very fascinated by the story herself. She provided me with a lot of information, and I read a couple of books about this girl and her strange disappearance. Then I decided to write about it.

In my book, it is a boy who disappears, and it's a completely different town and so on (The Ghost Town in the Sky really exists, and I saw it when I went skiing in Maggie Valley this winter). But some of the details, like the body floating in the creek long after she was killed, and not being decomposed at all, and the mother sitting in the window looking down when it floats by, stuff like that I kept similar to the real story. It's a truly fascinating unsolved mystery, and you can read more about it here:

https://northcarolinaghosts.com/coast/ghost-nell-cropsey/

I hope you enjoyed the book and that you'll leave a review if possible. Thank you for all your support.

Take care,

Willow

ABOUT THE AUTHOR

Willow Rose is a multi-million-copy best-selling Author and an Amazon ALL-star Author of more than 80 novels. Her books are sold all over the world.

She writes Mystery, Thriller, Paranormal, Romance, Suspense, Horror, Supernatural thrillers, and Fantasy.

Willow's books are fast-paced, nail-biting page turners with twists you won't see coming. That's why her fans call her The Queen of Scream.

Several of her books have reached the Kindle top 10 of ALL books in the US, UK, and Canada. She has sold more than three million books all over the world.

Willow lives on Florida's Space Coast with her husband and two daughters. When she is not writing or reading, you will find her surfing and watch the dolphins play in the waves of the Atlantic Ocean.

Tired of too many emails? Text the word: "willowrose" to 31996 to sign up to Willow's VIP text List to get a text alert with news about New Releases, Giveaways, Bargains and Free books from Willow.

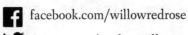

facebook.com/willowredrose

twitter.com/madamwillowrose

instagram.com/madamewillowrose

Published by BUOY MEDIA LLC
https://www.buoy-media.com

Cover design by Juan Villar Padron,
https://www.juanjpadron.com

Special thanks to my editor Janell Parque
http://janellparque.blogspot.com/

**To be the first to hear about new releases and bargains
from Willow Rose, sign up to be on the VIP List.** (I
promise not to share your email with anyone else, and I won't clutter
your inbox.)

- GO HERE TO SIGN UP TO BE ON THE VIP LIST :
http://readerlinks.com/l/415254

Tired of too many emails? Text the word: "willowrose" to

31996 to sign up to Willow's VIP text List to get a text alert with news about New Releases, Giveaways, Bargains and Free books from Willow.

FOLLOW WILLOW ROSE ON BOOKBUB:
https://www.bookbub.com/authors/willow-rose

Connect with Willow online:
https://www.amazon.com/Willow-Rose/e/B004X2WHBQ
https://www.facebook.com/willowredrose/
https://twitter.com/madamwillowrose
http://www.goodreads.com/author/show/
4804769.Willow_Rose
http://www.willow-rose.net
contact@willow-rose.net

CPSIA information can be obtained
at www.ICGtesting.com
Printed in the USA
BVHW070817080321
601990BV00004B/145